GLEN GR

Chicken Skin Tales

49 Favorite Ghost Stories from Hawai'i

MUTUAL PUBLISHING

Other books by Glen Grant...
Obake: Ghost Stories in Hawaii
Honolulu Mysteries: Case Studies in the Life of a Honolulu Detective
A Chilling Tale of Shave Ice: Mrs. Sugihara Haunts a Village
The Obake Casebook: Tales from the Darkside of the Cabinet
Obake Files: Ghostly Encounters in Supernatural Hawai'i

Library of Congress Catalog Card
Number: 98-68055

ISBN 1-56647-228-8

Design by Jane Hopkins
Cover illustration
and interior illustrations by Shane Johnson

First Printing, October 1998
1 2 3 4 5 6 7 8 9

Mutual Publishing
1215 Center Street, Suite 210
Honolulu, Hawaii 96816
Telephone (808) 732-1709
Fax (808) 734-4094
e-mail: mutual@lava.net
url: http://www.pete.com/mutual

Chicken Skin / Honolulu TimeWalks
2634 S. King St., #3
Honolulu, Hawaii 96826
Telephone (808) 943-0371
Fax (808) 951-8878
e-mail: chickenskin@compuserve.com
url: http://www.chicken-skin.com

Printed in Australia

TABLE OF CONTENTS

A WORLD OF CHICKEN SKIN
Where the Shadows Talk Back

C hicken Skin" is the sensation which sweeps over your body whenever you come close to the borderland between reality and mystery. It is the eerie feeling in your gut as your hair rises on the back of your neck, your flesh tingles with raised follicles, your heartbeat races and your eyes inexplicably water. When you experience "Chicken Skin," no measure of rationality or scientific objectivity can ease the overwhelming conclusion that beyond the material limits of life are unfathomable dimensions of the human experience that link our species to a world of unseen spirits. "Chicken Skin" reminds us that we still do live in a world where occasionally, the shadows do indeed talk back.

Perhaps our continued enjoyment of supernatural tales is only an ancient, genetic hope that our human personality will survive death. Maybe all ghosts and apparitions are as the skeptics claim, only the result of an electronic brain impulse or as Ebenezer Scrooge once surmised, "an undigested bit of beef, a blot of mustard, a crumb of cheese, a fragment of an underdone potato." Yet the "Chicken Skin" ghostly encounters in Hawai'i continue unabated. People of all ages, races, gender, educational and occupational backgrounds, and ethnicities continue to encounter the spirits of the dead. Ghost stories still circulate through word-of-mouth as Islanders continue to "talk story" into the wee hours of the morning, passing on family supernatural tales, sharing personal, uncanny experiences and keeping alive the centuries old tradition of legend-making.

Why do "Chicken Skin" ghost stories still persist in the Islands when the Age of Reason and Science should have long ago obliterated such ghostly lore as "humbug" and "balderdash?" A University of

Hawai'i astronomer has recently been quoted as saying that with the Hubbell telescope reaching into the farthest regions of the universe, "I have not seen any gods, ghosts or goblins. They are all part of the human imagination."

If such is the case, why do Islanders of all races continue to bless their houses and businesses before taking occupancy? Why are *ti* plants carefully planted around certain places considered sacred or sometimes "haunted?" Why is the *pikai* ceremony, or ritual sprinkling of Hawaiian salt, still performed for people or places bothered by restless ghosts? Certain words come to mind which are often used to explain such daily behaviors and experiences—"superstitious," "quaint cultural customs," "ignorance," "popular delusions."

However, the popularity of supernatural lore in Hawai'i is far more complex than is implied by the critics who label such beliefs as simply "unfounded and childish." While the Hubbell telescope may not be recording the existence of gods, ghosts or goblins, to find such entities the device may be pointed in the wrong direction—the mystery of the spirit realm is not unraveled by pointing our scientific tools in an outward direction. The answers are better found, perhaps, through an inward search—into the indelible mysticism of the human heart which shapes religious belief, alters physical reality and opens a door to the unknown regions of death. No telescope has ever been invented which can peer into this netherworld—no theory can ever explain the true heart of the matter. As Shakespeare said, "There are more things in heaven and earth, Horatio, / Than are dreamt of in your philosophy."

So Hawai'i's "Chicken Skin" stories persist as a living spiritual tradition of open-hearted and free-minded Islanders who know intuitively that the spirits of the ancient people have not wholly left the *'aina*, the land, which they once in life loved so dearly. In addition, the family spirits of the many immigrant cultures of Asia, the Pacific, Europe and the Americas which came to Hawai'i added to this supernatural mixed plate. Modern Islanders of various backgrounds continue to sense the presence of these ancestors in graveyards, family shrines or at special annual ceremonies honoring the dead such as the Japanese *Obon* festival, Chinese *Ching Ming* or Catholic All Soul's Day. With a powerful cultural tradition of supernaturalism perpetuated within the Native Hawaiian community, every new immigrant group has incorporated elements of the indigenous beliefs into their own mystical world of ghostlore.

Although through the generations some of these traditions have changed or waned, among the younger generation a persistent respect for the ghostlore of their parents and grandparents has amazingly survived in the face of modernization and skepticism. While the national popular culture has helped to keep alive an interest in the "unknown" through television series such as *The X-Files* or blockbuster films such as *Ghost*, Hawai'i's youth still draws heavily upon the unique quality of "local" supernaturalism, the traditions of Native Hawaiians and the *obake* or ghosts of Asia. As Island society undergoes tremendous socio-economic and political changes at the end of the twentieth century, it is heartening that the spiritual openness which is so often decried by the narrow-minded as "superstition" will definitely survive into the third millennium.

This collection is a small sampling of some of the favorite tales which I have collected from people of all walks of life in over three decades of studying Hawai'i's ghostlore traditions. Forty-nine ghost stories were selected because it is a Japanese supernatural belief that 49 is the number of days the spirit of the recently dead wanders among the living before passing over into the otherworld. While a few of the stories have appeared in my previous publications *Obake: Ghost Stories of Hawai'i* or *Obake Files: Ghostly Encounters in Hawai'i,* they are retold or in some cases updated here in the context of other ghostly encounters, that taken as a whole, represent the true multicultural uniqueness and spiritual power of Island people. As personal experiences originally shared by word-of-mouth, the stories in this collection are further evidence that Island legends are alive—they are not only ancient tales to be kept in an archive for the enjoyment of purists. The beauty of folklore is its living, organic nature. Just by recording and publishing these tales, the process of storytelling is empowered as these stories will find themselves being read, retold and reinterpreted around late night campfires, on back porch lanai or wherever Islanders gather to "talk story." And with any good, true tale—one story leads to another and then another and then another until a collective power transforms myth into cultural reality.

To enhance this process, all the stories told here have been written in a way to capture as much as possible the oral form of storytelling. In some cases, the stories are simply edited transcriptions of tales which are on audio recordings. Unlike tales written for a literary purpose, folklore material possesses a simplicity of language, a rhythm of plot and a sincerity of purpose which goes to the heart of why ghost stories are among the most popular genre of narrated tales. If there is any doubt over that assertion, the reader is invited to attend the National Storytelling Association's Annual Storytelling Festival in Jonesboro, Tennessee. The largest attended program during the two day event is the late night ghostly tales told in a graveyard which attracts over 10,000 listeners!

The sources for the tales are varied. Some of the stories come from the Japanese-American ghostlore project conducted in the 1970's in the American Studies Department of the University of Hawai'i. In the 1980's, a number of stories were collected from senior citizens throughout the State of Hawai'i through the Kapi'olani Community College, Office of Community Services senior citizen folklore project. Since 1991, when I commenced the "Ghosts of Old Honolulu" walking tour and other supernatural programs with Honolulu TimeWalks, I have been collecting numerous tales from individuals who have participated in these journeys through the lore of the Islands. A few stories have also been shared by listeners of the weekly "Chicken Skin: The Radio Show" and "The Grant Files" radio storytelling programs on KCCN 1420AM. I thank, Jayson and Julie Balanay, Charlie Doremus, Helen Fujie, Toni Hall, Masayoshi Hieda, and Cheryl Wilson for sending in their fascinating personal tales which I requested for inclusion among my forty-nine favorite stories. Finally, some of the stories shared here are based upon my own personal experiences with what in retrospect I believe were glimpses into the world of Chicken Skin. It is for each reader to decide what elements of these stories may or may not be genuine encounters with the spirits of the otherworld.

Every publishing endeavor invites a score of tributes to the individuals who have shared their talents, skills, stories and resources to make this collection of ghostly tales possible. First there is the consortium of talented people with whom I have been privileged to work in the past few years. Through the collective effort to pool our talents, energies and resources, we have all been able to expand our creative offerings. My deep-felt appreciation is thereby extended to "da Mo'ili'ili Blind Fish Tank" gang which includes James Grant Benton, Arnold Hiura, Audrey Muromoto, Jill Staas and Wilma Sur. There is no greater pleasure than the act of creation in the company of talented, loving friends.

Mahalo is also extended to Bennett Hymer and Jane Hopkins of Mutual Publishing Company who have supported all of my writing efforts with patience, enthusiasm and creative professionalism. The stunning cover illustration for this publication was produced by a young artist by the name of Shane Johnson. A fan of Chicken Skin tales, Shane's vivid imagination and artistic skill has added a welcomed dimension of supernatural surrealism to this presentation.

Finally, I wish to thank you, the *obake* readers of Hawai'i for the enthusiastic support which you have given to my work in the last decade. Being a storyteller and writer who loves to dip into the world of the arcane, there is a natural tendency by some to view these otherworldly collections as "superficial," "commercial" or "trivial." The warm support you have given me illustrates that these tales go deeper than some will allow—they are touching something within the soul of Hawai'i. My intentions have always been simple: I record, preserve and tell the supernatural lore of the Islands because I love ghost stories. You obviously share this love or you would not be holding this book in your hand. Ultimately then, you are my only important critical audience. Together, we are on this unending, mystical journey through the world of Chicken Skin. And I thank you.

Mo'ili'ili Blind Fish Tank
August, 1998

Pele at Sandy Beach

wo young local Japanese men were getting drunk in Waimanalo at a party they attended in the summer of 1949. As the party started to wind down, they recklessly decided it was time to drive back to their homes in Kaimuki. As drunk as they were, they should have slept off their revelry in Waimanalo. Instead, they jumped into their roadster and started the long drive back into town.

They had to make a decision about which way to go back to Kaimuki. Should they drive over the old Pali road at 1:30 a.m. in the morning? Having heard all type of stories about fireballs, ghosts and strange things appearing on that old winding road over the Ko'olau, they decided that way was too spooky. So instead they decided to take the south road which passed through Makapu'u and Sandy Beach, an area where they had heard of no ghost stories.

The driver revved up his engine and sped off on the narrow two-lane road, weaving drunkenly all over the highway. Fortunately, no one else was driving on the lonely, empty road at that early hour in the morning. Both of them were drinking beer as the passenger played his *ukulele*, loudly singing off tune. They passed Makapu'u beach, rose up the long incline to the top of the hill by the lighthouse access road and then sped down toward Sandy Beach when something appeared in the headlights, moving out into the road.

The driver slammed on his brakes as he and the passenger lurched forward, coming finally to a full stop. In their headlights they saw an elderly Hawaiian woman who had stepped into the road with her hands held up high above her head, signaling them to stop.

"What in the hell is she doing out here," the passenger asked, instinctively rolling up his window.

The elderly Hawaiian woman was wearing an old *mu'umu'u* with a dead *maile* leaf *lei* draped around her neck. She also had on an old-style Chinese straw hat which was adorned with a feather *lei* around the brim. Her white-and-gray hair hung down below her shoulders. They saw that she was barefoot as she walked up toward their car. Her face was kindly but ancient.

She approached the passenger's side of the car and tapped on the window he had just rolled up tight. He lowered it just a slight crack as she spoke to the two slightly frightened young men.

"Can we help you, Auntie," said the passenger shyly.

"I need a ride, boys," she answered in a cracked, old voice. "Can you give me a ride?"

The driver gestured a firm "no," as the passenger thought fast.

"Where you going, Auntie?"

"Waialua," was her simple response.

"Oh, sorry!" he exclaimed, now having a way out of having to give her a ride. "We are only going to Kaimuki. Maybe someone else will come along to give you a ride." He motioned to the driver to speed off. The clutch just started to be lifted off the floorboard, when the passenger's door, which he had forgotten to lock, opened.

"I'll go to Kaimuki," she said, starting to get into the car.

The young men had now no choice. They could hardly refuse the elderly woman her simple request. However, the passenger decided that he wasn't about to simply slide over in the front and give her the window seat. No way! If he had to sit next to the old, spooky woman, so would his friend! So he got out of the car and allowed her to slide across the front seat. The three of them together now sped off toward Sandy Beach, the drunken driver continuing his dangerous and erratic maneuvering of the highway. The elderly woman seemed undisturbed by their drunken behavior as she sat silently between the two young men.

As they approached the stretch of road along Sandy Beach, the elderly woman finally spoke.

"*Paka?*" she asked. "Smoke?"

"Sure, Auntie," the passenger answered, offering her a cigarette from the package in his shirt pocket. He dug into his pants to find her a match.

"*A'ole pilikia,*" she said softly. "No trouble."

She evidently didn't need a match as both men looked over towards her. Was she going to just suck on the cigarette? She certainly had no matches of her own to light the tobacco.

They watched as she placed the cigarette in her mouth, drew her two hands together in a gently cupped shape and then looked into her flesh. Slowly a red glow appeared in the depths of her hands, a glow that became more intense and brighter as the front of their car seemed to be illuminated in its radiating heat. She lifted her cupped hands to the tip of her cigarette, and took a deep drag as the smoke filled her lungs. Her palms cooled as she lowered her hands, puffed on the cigarette and then leaned back into the seat letting out the smoke with a slight, *kolohe* or rascal smile on her face.

Watching all of this in silent wonder, the passenger dropped his beer and *ukulele,* slowly moving himself away from the old woman as far as he could as he pressed his body against the car door, fixing his eyes upon his feet. The driver was suddenly cold, stone sober as he looked straight ahead to the highway as he repeated a silent mantra to himself: "Get to Kaimuki, get to Kaimuki, get to Kaimuki, get to Kaimuki."

They passed Halona or the blowhole without anyone saying one word in the car. The silence continued as the three drove past Koko Head crater and through the valleys of Maunaloa, Kuliouou, Niu, Aina Haina, Kahala and finally to a taxi stand at Waialae and 12th Avenue. When they stopped behind a taxi with its driver sitting on a nearby bench, the two young men leaped out of the car. The elderly Hawaiian woman slowly climbed out after them as they excitedly pointed to the taxi driver.

"Auntie," the driver said, "you see that man? He'll take you to Waialua. He'll take you wherever you like go."

"Oh, *mahalo,* boys," she said kindly. "You are so nice."

"Yeah, Auntie," added the passenger. "No problem."

"Good night," both of them called out to the old woman who walked over to the waiting taxi driver. They didn't look back as they drove off down Waialae Avenue to their homes.

"Did....did...you...see," the passenger finally started to ask the driver, mustering his courage, "what she..."

"SHUT UP!" yelled the driver, his eyes still fixed on the road. "Call me tomorrow!"

He didn't want to talk about what they had seen at night, but preferred the bright sun of daylight to confirm that they had both watched that elderly woman light her cigarette with nothing but the flesh of her hand!

The next evening they tracked down the taxicab driver who had been waiting to take the Hawaiian woman to Waialua. They anxiously asked him if she had done anything "spooky" or unusual during her ride to the North Shore. He looked puzzled by their question.

"What old woman?" he finally asked.

"The one we dropped off here last night," they answered. "The one wearing the old *mu'umu'u* and the old Chinese hat with the feather *lei*. Remember? We dropped her off here last night?"

"I remember the both of you," the driver confirmed, "but there was no old lady in your car. You two guys were alone."

"What?"

"You got out of the car, spoke to something that wasn't there, pointed at me and drove off. I figured you were just a couple of drunks. So what are you talking about this old woman?"

For many years those two men pondered what had happened to them that night at Sandy Beach. Who had been the woman in their car? Although neither man was Hawaiian, they could only come to one conclusion: that Pele the ancient goddess of the volcano, had stopped their car that evening on the road to Kaimuki. She had gotten into the automobile and lit the cigarette with her hands for the purpose of slightly scaring both of them so as to sober them up. For they realized that if they had sped drunk along that road to the rising, twisting section of the highway by the Blowhole and Hanauma Bay, they would have probably plunged to their deaths. In their brash, thoughtless actions they had endangered their lives. Pele, however, had for some inexplicable reason saved the lives of these two young men on that lonely Sandy Beach road.

WHO IS RUTH MALAMA?

C hick'n Skin: Supernatural Tales of Hawai'i was a collection of supernatural stories aired on KGMB television in 1996 during the Halloween season. The story of Pele lighting a cigarette with her hands in the car of two young men at Sandy Beach was filmed by Scott Sorenson with the assistance of James Grant Benton and his son Kui Benton as the men, and the entertainer Leina'ala Heine as the Hawaiian woman. While I did the voice-over narration, the actually filming of the sequence was done without my participation. The final product was an artful rendition of one of my very favorite ghost stories from Hawai'i.

The very next morning after the production was aired on television, a gentleman called me excitedly with a question concerning the Pele story.

"How did you know about that telephone pole?" he queried. "I told my wife that was real chicken skin when I saw that utility pole!"

"What utility pole?"

"The pole you had the lady in white standing next to when she stopped the car!" he explained. This was followed by burst of short questions that left my head spinning: "How did you know about that place? And wow, she was wearing a white dress?

Do you know about that lady? Have you talked to the police? Did you know about the lineman?"

Sorting through his excited scatter-gun of questions and explanations, I finally figured out that Henry Williamson had been watching the television show the previous evening when he was shocked to see that the "phantom hitchhiker" played by Leinaʻala Heine was standing next to a very unusual utility pole. This exact same wooden pole along the side of the road to Sandy Beach had been the place where a very eerie event had taken place a few years earlier concerning a utility company lineman and a "lady in a white dress." Not only had Leinaʻala been standing right next to that pole, but she had also been wearing a long white *muʻumuʻu* in the television scene.

I finally answered his series of questions by disclaiming any knowledge of the utility pole, the lineman or even the color of the dress of the actress. In the original ghost story, the elderly Hawaiian woman was described by the two men as wearing an "old *muʻumuʻu*," not necessarily a white dress. The famous "lady in white of Makapuʻu" to which Mr. Williamson kept referring was not necessarily the same spirit entity who had performed a miracle in the automobile of two drunk men. Then I explained that I had not even been at the filming of the sequence, so that the placement of the "phantom hitchhiker" at that particular utility pole had been entirely coincidental.

Mr. Williamson seemed greatly deflated by my confession of ignorance. He had hoped that I would be able to clear up a mystery which for many years had bothered him—the mystery of the "lady in white" who he believed haunted the road near that utility pole. I was finally able to coax the full story from him, a strange tale of hallucination or visitation in Hawaiʻi's world of Chicken Skin.

A few years earlier, Mr. Williamson now was able to explain calmly, he was supervising some utility work in the new subdivisions of Kalama Valley. Powerful gusts of 60 mph winds had been snapping lines, and he had his crew working throughout the district trying to secure the downed lines. About 9:00 a.m. he received an emergency call from the company's main headquarters. A passing motorist had just called 911 emergency concerning an accident involving one of his lineman at Sandy Beach. The emergency operator called the police, an ambulance and the utility company. Mr. Williamson sped to the scene of the accident which was only a few minutes away.

When he arrived there, the lineman was lying on his back on a comfortable patch of grass about five feet away from the pole. He had evidently been working on the utility line when a gust of wind knocked him off balance. Fortunately his harness was secure, so that when he fell, he landed on his leg which was broken in seven different places. The man was in agony, but conscious when Mr. Williamson arrived.

"Get Ruth Malama's phone number," was the first thing the lineman said to him when he knelt by his side, to assure him that help was on its way.

"Who?"

"Ruth Malama. Get her phone number. I promised to take her to dinner. Get her number."

Obviously, the fellow was delirious. The ambulance arrived and he was rushed to Queen's Hospital Emergency as Mr. Williamson worked with the police to file the accident report. He told the policeman that the worker was lucky that his harness was secured when he fell or he could have landed on his head. Mr. Williamson also thought it was "true grit" that the man had unharnessed himself and then crawled over to the patch of grass where he had found him resting.

The next day, he went to visit his worker at the hospital to pay his respects. The man's leg was in a cast and he was still in great pain. As Mr. Williamson walked into the room, the poor fellow sat up.

"Did you get Ruth Malama's phone number?" he asked.

"Hey, who in the hell is this Ruth Malama?"

"The lady in white who helped me when I fell yesterday."

"What lady in white," Mr. Williamson asked, puzzled.

The lineman explained that when he had fallen off of the telephone pole, a lady in a white dress and with long, snow-white hair came over to him. She had evidently been walking in the air when she saw the accident and came to offer her assistance. Unhooking the harness, she had carefully moved him to the grassy patch of lawn where he rested, waiting for help.

"She held my hand and kept telling me everything was going to be all right," the man further explained. "The lady was a lifesaver. I told her that when I got better I was going to take her to dinner. She told me, 'no need,' but I insisted. I asked for her phone number but she wouldn't give it to me. Finally I asked for her name.

"'Ruth Malama,' she answered. 'People call me Ruth Malama.'

"At that moment," the worker concluded, "you came over. She let go of my hand and walked away. That's why I told you to get her phone number. I promised her a dinner. So did you get her phone number?"

Mr. Williamson had to explain to his worker that there was no woman in a white dress kneeling with him when he had driven up. There was no woman anywhere in the area. The man had been alone, his harness released and his body resting comfortably on a patch of grass.

A quick call to the police revealed that the "lady in white" was famous as a spirit in the area around Sandy Beach and Makapuʻu. A search through the phone book found no "Ruth Malama." Calling the various families named "Malama," he could find no such woman living anywhere in Honolulu.

"This has puzzled me for years, Mr. Grant," Henry Williamson said before finally hanging up the phone. "How had that guy unhooked his harness and pulled himself to that grass? If he really saw a lady in a white dress helping him, who was she? She wasn't there when I pulled up. I swear she wasn't."

Who is Ruth Malama?

THE LOST LITTLE GIRL OF MANOA VALLEY

T here was a light rain falling over the back of Manoa Valley the evening in 1970 that John Murakawa answered the persistent call of his dog to go for its usual night-time stroll. Since his house is located near the Chinese cemetery in the back of the valley, he usually took Kipo down past the old graveyard before circling home. Clutching his umbrella in one hand and the tugging leash in the other, John was pulled by his dog into the unpleasant, damp darkness of the Manoa night.

At the corner near the westside of the graveyard, Kipo stopped to "do his business" along the curb. On the other side of the cemetery wall was an area of graves known as the "baby" section. These graves were reserved for infants about six years of age and younger. In Chinese tradition, it is believed that these young spirits need each other's companionship in the other world. A stroll through the "baby" section of the Chinese cemetery is a sad and poignant experience at any time of day. In the late evening, when the rain is falling to the light cry of the wind, this area can be downright chilling.

At first John thought that the cries he heard come from the graveyard was the valley wind blowing through the trees. But the persistent sobbing became more human as he realized that these sounds came from a child—a child who was in the cemetery. Peering over the wall, he was somewhat relieved to see that indeed a little girl, only six or seven years of age, was inside the cemetery, huddled under a tree behind one of the tombs seeking shelter. She was getting soaking wet in the rains that blow down the valley.

"What are you doing in there?" he asked her. In the faint light from the street lamp, he could see that she was a small Asian girl with long black hair. Her simple *aloha*-print school dress was soaking wet as was her light blue sweater.

"Where do you live?" he called to her. She didn't answer but continued crying. She was obviously frightened and apparently lost. John assured her that he wasn't going to hurt her. He only wanted to help her. When he walked over toward her, Kipo suddenly started barking and pulling away on the leash. John lost his grip on the wet leather as the terrified animal ran off, making a bee-line for home.

"What are you doing out here at night, little girl?" he asked kindly as he leaned down, putting his jacket over her wet body. She was trembling in the cold, damp night. "Won't you tell me your name?"

"Eily," she said between sobs, "Eily Kang. I live at 3578 Gulick Ave. I'm five years old." John thought how cutely she had recited her name, address and age as if she had practiced it for adults.

"Well, Eily Kang," John said cheerfully, "why don't we get you to someplace that is dry! You are going to catch your death of cold out here."

The rain had let up as the two of them walked out of the graveyard, hand-in-hand for the stroll back to his home. Along the way he asked her what she had been doing out there in the graveyard at night. Eily explained that earlier that after she had been visiting her cousin in Manoa. The cousin had invited Eily to join her friends in a game of hide-and-go-seek. Eily had run into the cemetery to hide, but nobody had come to find her. Even after sunset, she stayed in her hiding place until finally it started to rain. Then she got frightened, but she couldn't remember where her cousin lived. So she hid near the tomb under the protection of the tree.

When John got back to his home, he gave Eily a towel to dry off with as he had his wife look up the Kang family listing in the telephone book. Her parents must be frantic, he thought, looking for their daughter. There were over 100 Kangs in the directory, but none of them on Gulick. The simple solution, of course, was to simply drive her home.

"What's wrong with Kipo?" his wife asked.

"Nothing. Why?"

"He ran back here barking and yelping. That crazy dog is hiding under the bed."

"I don't know," John said. "Maybe he saw a mouse."

Eily Kang finished her glass of milk and then got into the back seat of John's car where she curled up under a warm blanket. In a short time, John was slowly cruising down Gulick Ave. looking for the address which the little girl had so proudly given him back in the cemetery. As he pulled into the driveway of the home, he remarked to himself how quiet and dark the house seemed. He had expected police cars and a set of very anxious parents frantically looking for their missing daughter. Maybe Eily Kang had given him the wrong address.

Leaving her behind sleeping soundly in the back seat, John went to the front door of the modest Kalihi home. It was after 11:00 P.M. when he knocked loudly on the door. A light in the back of the house turned on and a few moments later a man's voice spoke from behind the door.

"Who is it?"

"I'm sorry to bother you," John said, "but does Eily Kang live here?"

"What?" asked the voice behind the door. "What are you talking about?" The porch light turned on suddenly as the door creaked open a few inches and an elderly man peered out at John.

"Hi. My name is John Murakawa. I live in Manoa Valley, and tonight I found a lost little girl in our neighborhood. She gave us this address. Her name is Eily Kang."

"Is this a joke?" the man asked. He was joined by his wife who was talking excitedly in the background.

"No, not at all. Do you know her? Do you know Eily Kang?"

"Yes. She's our daughter. But you couldn't have found her in Manoa."

"Well, I did," insisted John. "She's in the back seat of my car right now."

"Our daughter died thirty years ago," the wife now blurted out. "I don't think this is funny at all."

"What?" John asked, puzzled. "Died thirty years ago? Then who's in my car?"

When John brought the parents out to the car to met the little girl named Eily Kang whom he had found in the Chinese cemetery of Manoa, the mysterious child had vanished from the back seat as had the blanket in which she had been wrapped. It took some serious explaining to the angry couple to convince them that he was not playing some malicious trick. He told them in detail how he had found the wet and frightened child in the cemetery.

"Our Eily is buried in the Manoa graveyard," the mother said quietly. Tears started flowing down her cheeks.

It was after midnight when John and the Kang family gathered at the site in the Chinese cemetery where he had met the little lost girl. The tomb she had been hiding behind was about thirty feet from the place where a child named Eily Kang had been buried on April 3, 1939. The air was now crisp as a half-moon peeked out behind a few passing clouds. The elderly couple were praying, placing an offering of candy on their long-departed child's grave and weeping in remembrance of a life that had been cut far too short. How empty their lives had been without Eily, their only child who did not grow up into adolescence, who did not attend college and marry that handsome young man and give them grandchildren to comfort them in the twilight of their lives.

Could it have really been the child from the grave who had been in his car? She had been so real! John felt more puzzled and skeptical than disturbed by the events of the evening. He felt uncomfortable in the presence of the grieving parents so he stepped away to be alone with his own thoughts. The Manoa wind now picked up as he pulled his jacket closer around him to fight the chill. It was then that it caught his eye, an unusual object laying on the grass not three feet behind the tomb of Eily Kang.

His neatly folded blanket was resting there among the graves of the dead.

A LADY IN WHITE AT SHERWOOD FOREST

I was walking out of the Kawaiahaʻo graveyard in downtown Honolulu one evening following a "Haunted Honolulu" walking tour when a policeman driving by in one of those motorized carts stopped me.

"Hey, what were all those people doing in the cemetery?" he asked politely.

"We just finished a tour," I replied as sincerely as possible so that he didn't mistake us for graverobbers.

"The ghost tour?" he said with a smile on his face. "I heard about that. Do you tell them about the lady in white at Makapuʻu Beach?"

I asked him how he knew about the lady in white, a well-known spirit that haunts the area on the southeast end of Oʻahu which is famed for swimming, body-surfing, fishing and a stunning vista.

"I've never seen her," he volunteered, "but I've talked to several of the guys who patrol that area. They've seen her. I understand they even have a log on her, a listing of all the sightings that have been reported."

Whether such a "spirit log" truly exists on the "lady in white," I have no idea. But judged by the number of stories which I've collected concerning her legendary appearance, it would seem that the Makapuʻu district is famed for this tantalizing spirit whose presence is often sudden and mysterious. Several people have reported that as they were driving in the early hours of the morning along the road that winds past Makapuʻu, they have seen a woman wearing a white dress along the side of the road. Sometimes she has been seen with a white dog. Then, just as you pass by her, she dashes in front of your car, vanishing right in front of your eyes.

Other people have seen her running along the Makapuʻu beach. As she runs along the wet shoreline, she leaves no footprints in the sand. On some occasions, she has been seen naked in the waters of Makapuʻu, calling out into the night the name of the lone fisherman casting out his lines—calling him into the still, cold darkness of the sea, enticing him to join her in the realm of death and mystery.

One late night in the 1950's, four Farrington High School friends were walking along the shoreline at Makapuʻu. As three of them ran off ahead, the fourth friend lagged behind looking for crabs that scurried across the sand at night. A piercing scream suddenly broke the stillness of the night, as the three young men turned around to watch horrified as their buddy was literally floating in the air! His body was being lifted up and into the sea as waves suddenly engulfed him, his screams now drowned out as he was pulled down into the dark waters of Makapuʻu. Then an instant later, a crashing wave delivered him up, drenched and gasping to the beach.

"Where in the hell is that wahine?" he was screaming as he struggled to his feet. "I'll kill her! Where is she?"

"What lady?" his stunned friends replied.

"The one that dragged me into the ocean! I'll kill her. Where in the hell did she go?"

It took an hour of arguing to convince their very wet and frightened friend that there had been no woman on the beach that night. Still he insisted that a young Hawaiian girl in a long white dress had suddenly come out of the surf, grabbed him from the shoreline, lifted him up and thrown him into the crashing surf, and then tried to pull him down into the water. Fortunately an in-coming wave helped him break free of her grip, carrying him to safety on the beach.

Here was a fellow who had actually been assaulted by the lady in white.

Who is this mysterious resident of Makapuʻu beach? While her identity may remain forever elusive, many years ago, there was a *pohaku* or rock that was located on the cliffs right below the lighthouse at Makapuʻu. This rock was shaped like the torso of a woman and was believed to be imbued with a female spirit named Malei. Oral traditions note that during the construction of the lighthouse, one of the workers kicked that rock into the ocean. The sacred *pohaku* Malei was forever lost. A few years later, the high intensity light exploded, killing the keeper of the lighthouse. This was the only such fatality in the history of lighthouses in Hawaiʻi. Had Malei sought out her revenge?

The lady in white of Makapuʻu continues to be sighted on the road from Halona, or the blowhole, to as far away as Sherwood Forest near Bellows Beach in Waimanalo. In July of 1996, a group of three men were driving home from Kailua to Hawaiʻi Kai. At approximately 11:30 p.m. they were passing the ironwood trees at Sherwood Forest, just by the area where the polo field is located. Their headlights noticed an elderly woman in an old-fashioned white *muʻumuʻu* standing dangerously close to the edge of the highway. Sitting beside her was her large white dog. The collar of her dress was stiff and buttoned in a style common in the last century. Her hair was long, white and stringy. She didn't seem to be intending to cross the road, but was standing there with her right hand oddly raised as if she was striking a pose with her two fingers holding a cigarette. Approaching her, they slowed down not knowing whether she intended to step into the road. They all noticed that although it seemed that she was holding a cigarette in her fingers, they could see no such object in her hand.

What in the world was she doing?

Just as they passed her, she suddenly bent down, turned and stared straight into their automobile with a gleeful, sinister smile! The driver's heart fluttered as his foot hit the gas and the other passengers screamed. The car lurched forward as they excitedly looked back on the strange old woman who had scared them.

To all of their amazement, there was no old woman standing on the side of the road. There was no white dog. The two figures had vanished.

A Haunted Affair

There are many other tales of hauntings at Makapuʻu. One of them concerns a lighthouse construction worker who had come with his wife from California to work on the federal project back in 1917. In the course of his living in Hawaiʻi, he had become involved with a local island girl. His adulterous affair lasted for several months until his wife discovered his infidelity. A terrible argument occurred the night she confronted her husband with the truth, demanding that he sever his affair immediately. He refused, asking for a divorce.

Driving away from their cottage, the distraught wife drove recklessly into the night. Perhaps it was the tears in her eyes that blurred her vision on the curving, steep road which at that time was still unimproved. Her car bounced against the side of the rocky cliff, went out of control and then careened over the ledge. When she was found, she was still alive but horribly burned. A few days later she died at Queen's Hospital with one dying message on her lips.

"Tell Tom, I'm coming back for him."

Several months later, Tom was driving the same road when his car suddenly turned and went over the embankment, plunging him to his untimely death. Had the accident been an unfortunate coincidence? Had Tom caused the accident himself through guilt? Or had the jilted wife won her final revenge?

Turn the clock forward to 1980. A Hawaiʻi Kai resident was driving his car by Makapuʻu Beach one evening at about 11:00 P.M. when he suddenly had a blow-out to one of his rear tires. Pulling over as close as he safely could to the railing, he got out to change the tire. As he unscrewed the lug nuts on the wheel, he placed them into the inverted hubcap which rested next to him.

When the last lug nut was thrown into the hubcap, he suddenly heard a metallic rattling. Looking down, he noticed that the lug nuts were moving about in the hubcap, one of them actually floating! The man was mesmerized by this incredible poltergeist taking place right before his eyes! Mesmerized, that is, until he felt something tingling on either side of his neck. Then he was frozen with fear. The ice cold fingers of two hands were touching the sides of his neck!

Quickly brushing the hands away, he turned, falling back to the pavement. Standing above him was a woman in a white dress, her outstretched hands reaching down toward him like a lover seeking an embrace. Although the woman's face was partly obscured by her long, dark brown hair blowing across it in the night, he could see that her cheeks, nose and mouth were horribly charred and blackened. One eye socket appeared grossly empty, the burned skin about her eyes hanging like strips of seared wallpaper. And then from her burned mouth, words were spoken as if from the depth of a bottomless well.

"Tom? Tom?" She reached down to embrace her lover with a kiss upon his insanely shrieking mouth.

He didn't stop running until a mile later when he collapsed to the side of the road, questioning what he had just seen as a waking nightmare. Tomorrow he would have his wife drive him out to Makapuʻu to pick up his abandoned car. In fact, he thought to himself as he walked the rest of the way home to Hawaiʻi Kai, he would pay a lot more attention to his wife. And his affair with the woman at the office would just have to stop. He pledged to himself that he would be forever faithful to his vows of marriage.

For the cheating husband had learned a very special lesson in a very hard way. If a man who is committing adultery drives the road along Makapuʻu beach, he may be stopped by a lady in white who in death still seeks out the man who done her wrong.

A Fireball at Kaunakakai

E dith Kamakaala was sitting on her front porch at her home in the town of Kaunakakai, Moloka'i in 1978 enjoying the evening air. Looking out into the northern sky on a cloudless evening, she marveled at the millions of stars that twinkled in the heavens. Tiny silver dots of burning comets soared light years away.

Then from the dark horizon, one of these burning comets rose as if from the land itself, its fire soaring bright and reddish-yellow as it made its ascent into the sky above Kaunakakai. As this ball of fire arched up overhead, she watched its tail extend halfway across the evening sky as this afterglow turned bright yellow, then dimmed to a burning red. While other shooting stars crisscrossed the outer limits of the universe, this fiery comet scorched the earth's atmosphere. In fact, from what Edith could determine, this fireball was actually soaring only several hundred feet off the ground.

This was no comet, she now knew. The fire in the night was what her *tutukane* had once described to her many years before when she was a small *mo'opuna* or grandchild. She was watching an *akualele*, a flying god, light the evening sky above Moloka'i. Although her *tutukane* had told her that these fireballs were death-rendering creations of people wishing to do harm to others, she watched transfixed as the fire cackled over her house and then spun out with a whistling sound to the gymnasium of the school in Kaunakakai where that evening a dance was being held.

When the *akualele* reached the school building, it suddenly seemed to hover, suspended in air for just a moment. Circling around the school grounds, the fireball seemed to almost be listening to the disco music which blared through the windows and doors of the gymnasium. Then the malicious fire turned back toward Edith's home, shot skyward like a roman candle and then plummeted back to earth. The missile struck directly the top of the neighbor's roof, vanishing in an instant. There was no explosion, no flames, no splintering wood, no sound. The heavens returned to peace with their millions of sparkling planets and stars as Edith retreated inside to her room to be comforted by the Psalms of the Holy Bible.

In the morning she was not surprised to learn that the old man who lived next door in the house struck by an *akualele,* had died in his sleep during the night. She never told his family what she had seen, but for many months she was troubled by many disturbing thoughts.

Who had sent that fireball of death to take the life of that harmless old man? Had it wanted one of the children from the school? And God forbid, would it ever return?

The *Obake* Church of Waialua
As Told by Julie and Jayson Balanay

S t. Michael's Catholic Church lies in ruins not far from Thomson's Corner in the district of Waialua on the island of O'ahu. Rising like tombstones from the land once covered in canefields, this interesting historic site is very visible as one drives to the North Shore on Kaukonahua Road along the base of the Wai'anae mountains. The church was constructed about 1852 by Father Joseph Devauz and his native Catholics who settled in the valley along the Kaukonohua Stream. Built of huge boulders which were laboriously hauled up from the stream, the walls of the massive structure were over three feet thick. Enormous stone buttresses were erected to support the lime-plastered stones which were also reinforced with a heavy chain anchor obtained from a sailing ship. The timbers for the interior rafters were fashioned from the *'ohi'a* trees which once flourished in the region. A three-story bell tower once rose in the front of this house of God which served the Catholic population of Waialua for over six decades.

In later years, the Hawaiian Catholics were joined in Mass at St. Michael's by the Portuguese families who had come to work at the huge Waialua Sugar Plantation. A school for Portuguese children was opened at the church as this religious complex became a lively cultural and spiritual center of the North

Shore. However, by 1912, the congregation of St. Michael's Catholic Church had fallen off as the Portuguese gradually moved elsewhere and the Hawaiian population dwindled. Then came a terrible fire which destroyed the old building, leaving only its haunted shell to mark the place where God had once been worshipped. In time the children of the district came to know the ruins as simply "*obake* church."

Today the ruins of this *Obake* Church and its quiet graveyard, which is sometimes still used for burial, are quiet and desolate. In its vicinity are several other hidden sites which remind the modern visitor that so much of Hawai'i's history remains neglected or concealed. Not far from the ruins is, for example, a *pohaku kapu* or sacred stone which in ancient times was located in Poloa grove. This stone was considered sacred to the goddess Pele and in the 1920's was identified by a thicket of breadfruit, mango and *kuku'i* trees. Many Hawaiian burials could be seen near the stone which was marked by an old iron fence erected by the plantation. A visitor in 1950 could find neither the sacred stone, the fence nor the burials.

Other ancient things have vanished from the area. Near the old sugarmill smokestack that rises in a field not far from Thomson's Corner, the remnants of Kahakahuna *heiau* once stood. This ancient temple has been completely destroyed as was the nearby Kawai *heiau*, located below the Waialua Plantation manager's house. The informed explorer however, may discover the remnants of an ancient irrigation ditch which is visible in sections through Kamananui, the plains that form along the Wai'anae range.

Why would the walls of the old ruined church still be standing, considering the value of the property in the early days for sugar production? One folk tale was told of how Mr. Thomson, the manager of the plantation, had first wanted to tear the old walls down. But then he had an unusual vision about the old church. One night in his dream, an angel instructed him to leave the church alone—the walls should be left standing. Although he was not a superstitious man, the manager had enough respect for Hawaiian supernaturalism to leave well enough alone. The walls, he ordered, were to be left untouched.

A *kupuna* or elder of Waialua shared a story with me about a group of three young Portuguese men who had gone pig-hunting in the hills above Waialua. They had caught and killed a 150-pound pig which they were bringing back home in the late afternoon along the cane haul road which passes the ruins of St. Michael's Catholic Church. They had wrapped the pig up in a gunny sack, tied the sack to a strong pole and shared the heavy load on the long trek back to Waialua. Since the pig was heavy, they took turns hoisting the load over their shoulders. As time passed, they each noticed that the weight of the pig got a little lighter. They credited this to the fact that they were strong young men and they were probably just getting used to the load. However, by the time they passed the Obake Church, the weight of the pig was amazingly light. They put the pole down and opened the gunny sack to check on their meat. To their complete wonderment, the pig had utterly disappeared, leaving not a trace! The spirits of the Obake Church, they later reasoned after they had fled the scene, had taken the pork as their own.

In 1982, a young woman who grew up in Waialua had an eerie encounter at the old Obake Church. An experienced horseback rider, Julie Balanay often explored the back country of Waialua, sometimes going as far as Ka'ena Point or *mauka* toward Schofield Barracks. However, on the advice of her grandfather, she had never really ridden near the ruins of St. Michael's Catholic Church. He hadn't said much about why to stay away from the area, but simply warned her not to take her horse near the old historic site.

One day she and her friend went horseback riding, but her friend wanted to take a different route from the one they usually followed. Instead of their normal routine which was around the beach, her friend wanted to go toward the mountain side. On the way out, they stopped by their friend's store to buy a soda and "talk story." The friend owned two dogs which were always hanging around the store. One of the dogs was a white shepherd and the other one was a regular "cow dog." These dogs were very used to being around horses. In fact, whenever the girls rode up, the dogs came out of the store and would actually greet the horses. This particular day, the store was crowded with customers. So Julie and her companion asked their friend if they could take the two dogs along on their trip into the mountains. The storeowner agreed, so the two riders, their horses and two barking dogs running behind, headed off along the winding road of Waialua to the back valleys of the Wai'anae range.

As they approached the cane haul road that leads past the Obake Church, her friend suggested they take the turn into the gravel-strewn road. Julie didn't say anything in protest, but she knew this was the place from which her grandfather had warned her away. Several barrels barricaded the road to prevent curious automobile drivers from entering the cane road and in the distance she could see the two big arches of the ruins rising from the ground. The mature sugarcane fields were blowing in a slight breeze when suddenly the otherwise sunny sky turned cloudy in seconds. The wind picked up into a whistling whine as they all passed the church. The hairs on the back of Julie's neck rose. Was it her imagination, or did she indeed feel the presence of some unseen entity? Then her horse came to a dead stop.

"What's wrong, boy," she said soothingly to her horse, petting his neck. The eyes of the horse, she noticed, were wide-open and almost bulging out of their sockets. His breath was quick and panting as if they had been in a full run, even though they had been walking. Something was definitely scaring her horse.

Just to the right, along the side of the road, she then noticed an old graveyard with several tiny baby cradles on a row of separate tombs. An overwhelming sense of the pitifulness of death now embraced her as she saw a tiny child's gown draped over a crudely-made stick cross. Another grave had baby rattlers placed on top of the mound. A pair of baby shoes were draped over another headstone. As fresh as these infant offerings were, the graves themselves seemed strangely neglected. Weeds grew irreverently over the ground where the infants were buried and many of the headstones were tipped over or broken. Julie's eyes watered as she thought about the emptiness of all these baby graves. The wind blew louder as if the cries of the infants were carried in this chilling breeze.

"Let's go back," she now urged her friend.

"Why?" answered her friend who was unmoved by the strangeness of the moment. "We aren't even halfway yet."

"This is unholy ground. I gotta go back. My grandfather warned me not to come here, and now I know why."

Since her friend could see the fear in Julie's face, she finally agreed to return to the main road. As they were turning their horses around, the wind suddenly gusted through the graveyard, knocking over several cradles. Her horse kicked, reared up and started snorting and whinnying. The "cow" dog barked frantically at this point, growling toward the graveyard while backing away as if it saw something among the tombs. The white shepherd was whimpering, crying like a baby, and then bolted past the barricade of barrels and ran off toward the store. The "cow" dog followed after its terrified companion.

Just as Julie thought she was able to calm her horse down, the panicked animal suddenly kicked again, throwing its rider to the ground. It raced down the road to the barricaded barrels, leaped over them and galloped off riderless into the distance.

"What's happening?" her now anxious friend asked.

Julie just shrugged, pulling herself onto the back of her friend's horse. "Let's just get out of here, now," she urged her friend.

They rode down to the barrels when their horse suddenly reared back as if it now saw something blocking the way. There was no way they could get the steed to go forward, so they rode it up a small dirt hill and out to the main road. About a mile down the road they found Julie's horse with the empty saddle on its back. The animal was still panting loudly from its frightening encounter. Further down the road they heard the water flumes of the plantation irrigation system mixed with barking. They found the white shepherd dog on the other side of the flume, hiding in a small shelter. Julie laid some planks over the flume so that the dogs could climb out. Reunited, the group went back to the store, arriving just before sunset. There they found the "cow" dog sitting peacefully in front of the building as if nothing ever happened to it.

While her girlfriend always insisted that she had felt nothing unusual at the *Obake* Church, Julie believed that the spirits of the graves had come forth to greet them that day in 1982. She never returned to that place, since the memory of her experience there never diminished. As the years passed and she grew into adulthood, it was the story she told her husband whenever they drove out to Waialua along the Kaukonahua Road to visit their families.

Her husband Jayson never doubted the spiritual truth of his wife's tale, but his curiosity to visit the graveyard next to the *Obake* Church was in time very enticing. It was now March, 1998 when Jayson and Julie returned to place where she had been so frightened as a little girl. It remained virtually unchanged, except that now there was a gun-firing range at the end of the cane haul road past the ruins of the church. As they walked about the area on a beautiful, sunny day, Julie pointed out all the places where her story had actually taken place.

As his wife started telling him the story again, he suddenly started feeling as if someone was watching them. Looking over the area, he was not surprised to see someone was observing them, an old Filipino man tending his vegetables in an old field beyond the graves.

"Eh, what you folks doing?" he asked.

"Oh nothing, *tata*," Jayson replied. "Just looking around."

"Okay, but if you folks are looking for the gun range," the Filipino man politely said, "it's all the way down into the valley."

They told him that they weren't looking for the gun-range— that they had come to visit the graveyard. The old man walked over to them with a smile on his face, eager to make conversation.

"You know this place," he said, "no like now. Was more nice, you know."

"Yes," Julie said. "And scary too."

When he heard that, he started telling the old plantation stories that surfaced around the area. He was telling them that he didn't know why they would put a gun range out there, because there were a lot of spirits in this area. It would be disrespectful to these ancestors, the old man explained.

Julie and Jayson nodded in agreement. They assured him that there must have been a good reason why somebody would have put a gun-range in that district. Finally after about fifteen minutes of sharing stories, the Filipino man said good-bye to the couple and they watched him walk off down the road as they returned to their exploration of the *Obake* Church.

A few minutes later, Jayson was standing in the place where the infant cradles had been sixteen years before. The graves were still there, but the toys and cradles had long vanished. As Julie recalled the many uncanny events of long ago, Jayson was beginning to imagine the voices of the baby's crying when he suddenly sensed another calling—the call of nature. Excusing himself, he went off to find a place of seclusion in the bushes to relieve himself. Along the way he came across a photograph which was tangled in the brush. Someone had evidently discarded it, or it had blown there from across the now empty fields where sugarcane once grew. He picked it up and was startled to see it was a photograph of the old Filipino man.

When Julie examined the photograph, she agreed that the man in the picture looked exactly like the old Filipino man with whom they had a few minutes before been sharing stories of the old days. He must have dropped it when he was getting his vegetables from the garden, Jayson thought. They both looked around to see if they could still see him, but he was long gone. Jayson stuffed the photo in his pocket as they continued to study the various gravestones.

At one of the graves, Jayson stopped dead in his tracks, the "chicken skin" rising on his arms and the back of his neck. For on the face of the stone tablet was a photograph embedded into the tomb. While this practice of placing a photograph of the dead on the gravestone was not uncommon in Hawai'i cemeteries, the photograph on this particular grave was highly unusual. It was the same picture of the old Filipino man that he had earlier stuffed into his pocket! The death date on the grave was clearly chiseled, "1924."

Julie confirmed that the man on the tomb was indeed the same Filipino man whom they had just met walking about the *Obake* Church grounds. Discretion being the better part of valor, the two of them made a quick exit, racing back to their automobile. They could sort all of this out at home. As they were getting into the car, they both heard a distinctive, familiar voice say into the wind one simple word.

"*Salamat*," the voice of the old Filipino man said. They both heard his kindly voice speak that word only once—"thank you" in Talagog.

Later that evening Julie and Jayson visited with his family in Waialua, sharing with his parents what had happened. His mother silently listened and then said that she believed the voice was the old Filipino man's spirit which had been restless and alone in that remote little graveyard. He had needed someone to talk to, and when he told them "*salamat*," before they left, his spirit must have felt very happy.

"Why would he be thanking us?" Jayson asked his mom.

"Because you went there," she explained, "and it was like you were visiting him in his grave so that is why he was thanking you. So you should not feel frightened, but be very happy."

For over 80 years the *Obake* Church has excited the imagination of Waialua residents, sparking tales of intrigue, mystery and the supernatural. For one young couple, Julie and Jay Balanay, the ruins of that old Catholic Church will be an unforgettable memory of a day they kept company with the dead and were blessed in return with his eternal gratitude.

When Greg Kalani Yee was a young boy in the sixties growing up in a small subdivision outside of Wailuku, Maui, "small kid time" consisted of playing in the neighborhood in the afternoon with his friends, hanging out at the local "mama and papa-san" store, enjoying shave ice, going to the beach with his uncle, and night-fishing with his Dad on the weekends. It was an absolutely normal childhood with only one small, strange detour into the world of Hawai'i's supernatural.

It began as a nightmare that plagued Greg when he was seven years old. He woke up in the middle of the night, disturbed by the sound of ancient Hawaiian drums in his closet. The drumming was followed by the thunder of marching feet behind the closed door, enough feet to easily make up a small army. The whole house seemed to vibrate as he sat up in his bed, watching scores of Hawaiian warriors pressing through his closet door, their bodies literally moving through the wood as their transparent forms knew no material barrier. Young Greg watched horrified as these men marched silently through his room, one after another, each one vanishing as they moved toward the wall. Scores of these ancient warriors came out of his closet until the last marcher appeared and then vanished. At that moment, the drums suddenly stopped, and the room became deathly still.

While seeing an army of warriors walking out of your closet would be reason enough to be terrified, the young boy was more horrified by their facial and bodily features. For these Hawaiian spirits did not resemble any human male that he had ever seen. Their bodies were broken, gnarled and twisted as if they had been mangled in some hideous accident. The grimaces upon their faces was equally hideous and tortured—they appeared like a gallery of demonic freaks whose pain was hellish and eternal. The long strands of their hair were matted, filthy clumps which stuck out in all kinds of strange and frightening ways.

The first time that he had the nightmare, he ran crying and screaming to his parents' bedroom. When they asked him what was wrong, he tried to describe what had happened in detail. His parents reassured him it was only a bad dream and the next night left a small lamp on the dispel his fears. The hideous marchers, however, returned that night, and the next and the next. Night after night he would have this reoccurring vision until finally his mother, convinced that her son's dreams may be a sign that their house was haunted, sought out the counsel of an elderly Hawaiian woman who was known on Maui for her spiritual powers.

When the Hawaiian woman visited the home, she immediately felt a spiritual disturbance throughout the entire subdivision which was focused in young Greg's bedroom. Performing the *pikai* ritual, or sprinkling of Hawaiian salt to purify the home, she explained that sometimes spirits of the past were trapped in the agony they experienced at the time of their deaths. The grotesque nature of their bodies, face and hair was a spiritual distortion of the suffering they felt in life. This was especially intense for these spirits, she said to the family, because the spirits marching through this house had died during a terrible battle.

"This area was a battleground?" Greg asked wide-eyed.

"Not exactly," answered the elderly spiritualist. "The battle actually took place in 'Iao Valley."

In the days of Kamehameha's wars to extend his control throughout the Hawaiian Islands, a great battle took place on the lands of Wailuku. Kamehameha and his chiefs landed their invading force in war canoes that covered the beaches from

Kahului to Hopukoa. The fighting was intense for two days as the Maui warriors fiercely defended their island. Finally, a foreign cannon manned by the *haole* advisors John Young and Isaac Davis was brought up to the battle by Kamehameha. The slaughter was horrible. The defending armies were pushed back up into a narrow pass in 'Iao Valley where the cannon bombarded them mercilessly. Having finally routed the Maui warriors who scrambled up the side of the steep cliffs to escape the torrent of the foreign weapon, Kamehameha ordered his men to pursue the vanquished defenders. The battle was thereafter known as Ka'uwa'upali ("clawed off the cliff") and Kapaniwai ("the damming of the waters") for the corpses of the dead were piled so high that the stream through 'Iao was dammed up. The waters turned to the color of blood.

"So Kamehameha fought right here where we live?" Greg again pressed the elderly Hawaiian woman for an answer.

"No," she carefully explained to his parents. "But after the battle, the bodies were left by the victors to bake in the sun. In time many of them washed out of 'Iao Valley, their bones finally coming to rest on this plain where they were finally buried by silt, mud and sand. Their remains are beneath your house and their spirits are restless and disgraced in death. The child can sense what adults cannot."

The blessing of the house by the Hawaiian spiritualist seemed to have helped. Greg no longer had the vision of the wild-eyed, tormented victims of the battle of 'Iao Valley walking through his bedroom. But the thought that their house was over this type of burial site was too disturbing to his parents, who moved away to another district on Maui.

As for the house, Greg sometimes takes a drive up to the subdivision to just cruise past the home. Over the years he's noticed that families move in and out of the house on a very short-term basis. Not having the courage to ask any of the occupants if they have experienced any untoward disturbances, he is resigned to carry that unanswered curiosity about them throughout his life. Yet on some quiet evenings in the moment before sleep, he still vividly recalls the closet door through which marched an army of defeated men, their tormented souls seeking pity through endless history.

THE BABY-SITTING SPIRITS

As Told by Toni Hall

When Nancy Baquering was about six months old, her father decided to have her blessed in the Filipino tradition. In this case, it meant a ceremony in which *compares* or godparents were chosen to speak for the child. Her father was a firm traditionalist who wanted his parents at the ceremony. Nancy's paternal grandparents, however, had died many years prior to her birth. A friend advised her father that there was a way to make sure that the spirits of the ancestors were present during the blessing. Several candles were lit in honor of his deceased parents and Nancy's father prayed to them, inviting them to the ceremony.

The blessing went off without any problems. All the friends and relatives of the Baquering family attended the ceremony at their small plantation home. The food, which included a large roast pig, was plentiful. Gifts were given to the baby as everyone admired this first-born child. Nancy's father was beaming with pride that day—all his expectations for a traditional ceremony had been met. He prayed that the spirits of his parents had been in attendance as late that night he and his wife finally were able to put little Nancy to bed in her own small room. A short while later, the happy parents went to sleep.

It was in the still dark hours of the next morning that Nancy's cries woke up her mother. She was about to get out of bed to tend to her infant when suddenly the baby started cooing, as if someone was coddling her. She laid her head back on the pillow, shutting her eyes with the thought that her husband had gotten up to take care of Nancy.

A moment later, she rolled over and noticed that her husband was actually still lying next to her, sound asleep. Afraid that the baby would start crying again, she got up to check on her infant. It was only a few short steps to Nancy's room. As she walked in, she was stunned to discover her child actually floating around the room! The infant was at chest height, as if an invisible person were holding her in their arms, gently rocking the baby. Screaming for her husband, she was frozen at the doorway unable to move as she watched the child float back to the bed, gently landing into place and instantly going to sleep.

Nancy's mother was frantic, convinced that an *obake* had come to steal her child. Despite all of the spiritual precautions that they took by placing Bibles, salt and *ti* leaves about the house, the next night the same thing occurred—Nancy woke up in the night crying as an invisible person held her in its arms, rocking her back to sleep. Was there no way to stop this unwanted spirit from touching her child? The strange occurrences continued night after night.

Finally, Nancy's father went to one of his Hawaiian friends who had a reputation in the community for being a *kahuna* or priest. He confided in the priest everything that had happened, explaining how none of their protections were working. His wife was a complete nervous wreck. The Hawaiian friend told him that since he had invited the spirits of his parents into his home, they would stay there until they were sent back to their own spirit realm. His friend instructed him to light candles on the home altar, thank his parents for their blessings on his child, and politely ask them to leave.

Exactly one month after the original ceremony, Nancy's father carefully followed his friend's instruction. Lighting the candles in the room with his baby in her bed, he solemnly thanked his parents for their visit and their blessings. But now was the time for them to leave, he insisted. They were frightening his wife. Tears poured down his cheeks as he spoke to his long-departed parents whom he loved and missed very much. As much as he wanted them to be near him, for the sake of the family they would have to leave.

Suddenly, the candles all blew out. A chilling, light breeze moved through the room as the sleeping baby began to make cooing sounds in her sleep. And then Nancy rose from her bed and gently floated into the arms of her weeping father. Two white mists streamed up from the floor, floated to the ceiling where they hovered for a moment before fading away.

ALOHA OE
As told by Cheryl Wilson

The funeral for my grandmother in the spring of 1950 was a beautiful memorial service held in a church in Kaimuki. My grandmother had lived a full life and left this world attended by her large, grieving family. She and my grandfather had been blessed with many children who bore them numerous grandchildren.

When the Mass was over, the final blessings were given to be followed by the procession out of the church. The six pallbearers were chosen to carry my grandmother to her final resting place. They solemnly gathered around her coffin, slightly bent their knees and gently lifted the side handles in precise unison. As all six of the men then attempted to rise up and take grandmother on her last journey, the coffin would not move. It seemed as if it were fastened down to the bier with bolts. Quickly glancing at each other in astonishment, they tried again to lift the coffin. Again grandmother's remains would not budge. Realizing now what strange occurrence was taking place, a murmur rose from the mourners in the church.

My grandfather knew instantly what was happening. Although he was a devout Catholic, grandfather was well-steeped in old Hawaiian beliefs concerning the spirits of the dead. When the coffin did not move, it was the Hawaiian understanding that the deceased was not ready to go because the loved ones were not there to say good-bye.

Now grandfather looked among the mourners to see if everyone my grandmother loved was in attendance. Her *punahele* or favorites were her *mo'opuna* or grandchildren. All of the grandchildren were at the funeral, grandfather knew, but my two older boy cousins were nowhere to be found. As the first grandchildren, they were especially favored by grandmother.

A quick search was made for the cousins and they were soon discovered outside, playing on the church grounds. The boys were ushered in to pay their respects and to bid a fond *aloha* to their beloved *kupuna*.

After the good-byes were said, the pallbearers lifted the coffin without any trouble. The procession followed my grandmother out of the church and then on to Diamond Head where she would eventually be laid to rest.

In her final farewell, my grandmother had taught her *mo'opuna* her last earthly lesson. The bond of *aloha* is not severed by death.

FROM OUT OF THE SKY IN KAHUKU

The *haole* or Caucasian woman whom I interviewed in 1973 was then about 45 years old. She explained that she was a telephone operator with Hawaiian Tel at the main offices in downtown Honolulu. Every night after work she would drive from Honolulu to Hau'ula at the far north end of O'ahu, a long but relaxing drive which she had actually begun to enjoy. That is, up until a few nights before when something inexplicable had taken place on the remote stretch of highway between the Turtle Bay Hilton Hotel and the Kahuku Sugar Mill.

Often skeptics ask me how can I discern the truth-teller from the leg-puller. Of course, I do not give my informants lie-detector tests. Nor do I challenge their facts or attempt to expose inconsistencies. As a collector of ghostlore, all stories are valid whether they are accurate, exaggerated, fabricated, imagined or passed on from the infamous FOAF ("friend of a friend"). However, if the storyteller is sharing a personal encounter with ghosts, the veracity of the tale is often determined by the demeanor of the narrator. The telephone operator's extreme nervousness, her watery eyes and shaking hands told me that whatever she had seen on the Kamehameha Highway in Kahuku that evening in 1973, she truly believed she had seen it.

The time was just about 2:00 a.m., she explained, as she drove the lonely highway past the exclusive north shore hotel. There were no cars at all on the road, none in front, behind or approaching. Her headlights were on high beam, showing nothing on the road ahead. The radio was getting only getting static, so she turned it off. Instead she rolled down her window to enjoy the cool air on a beautiful Hawaiian night. Her cruising speed was about 45 miles per hour. She was thinking that a cup of tea would be nice when she got home, then her car struck a pedestrian who had suddenly crossed the highway about a mile away from the sugarmill.

Petrified that she had just killed someone, she slammed on her brakes, the smell of burning rubber and squealing tires piercing the still, quiet night. Her car was going out of control as she tried to maneuver away from the embankment where she feared she would plunge into the sugar cane field. The victim had fallen down hard on the hood of her car, the poor woman's body rolling back to the windshield and then bouncing back to the hood. When would the car finally stop, a detached voice inside her head kept pleading. The victim again rolled back to the windshield, turning her face to the terrified driver.

There on the hood of the moving vehicle was a young Hawaiian girl wearing a long, green flowing dress. From the glow of the dashboard illuminating the front of the windshield, she could see that the girl wasn't much older than sixteen years of age. The look on her face was one of horror and disbelief. How horrible to kill someone, the telephone operator kept thinking as she looked right into the anguished face of the young victim. Then, just as the car came to a final stop, the girl on the hood lifted her head up on her elbow, peered right in at the driver, and changed her expression. A slight *kolohe* or rascal smile replaced the horror as she gave the driver a malicious wink with one eye.

Standing up to her feet on the hood of the stopped car, this young girl then jumped into the night sky. The telephone operator watched as her body trailed off into the nothingness of a still night.

Back From the Realm of the Dead

At Ka'ena Point on the northwestern tip of O'ahu, there is a huge white stone which rests along the shoreline. This rock is called *leina-a-ka-'uhane* or "the place where souls leaped into the nether world." Legends say that the spirits of the dead would gather on this rock and each one of them in turn would jump into a darkness that appeared on the horizon, entering that mysterious realm from which no traveler has ever returned. A few travelers, however, have been awfully close to telling us what it would have been like to enter this eternal night.

One such spiritual sojourner was an elderly Hawaiian woman whom I had the honor to interview at Waialua, O'ahu in 1985. She started off her story by noting that in 1949 she had died on the island of Kaua'i. Adjusting my hearing, I apologized and asked her to repeat herself.

"You have heard correctly," she said, smiling. "I died in 1949."

Having been ill for several days at her family home on Kaua'i, she told me how as a young woman she had finally succumbed to the sickness. At the moment of death, she recalled how her spirit rose from her body and hovered at the ceiling of the room. She watched as her family grieved about her dead body, and she felt an urge to leave the room and journey across the channel from the island of Kaua'i to O'ahu.

When she arrived on the island of Oʻahu, she stepped on the beach at Mokuleʻia where she saw the spirits of the *ʻaumakua*, the guardian angels, existing side-by-side with the living. The mortals she noticed seemed wholly ignorant of the fact that spirits watched over them, protecting and caring for them. Then she saw how other spirits who had recently died were gathering at Mokuleʻia. She felt a loving desire to join them in a long, solemn procession to Kaʻena Point.

As the spirits of the recently deceased approached the end of the island, they came to this great white rock along the shoreline. One at a time, each soul climbed the rock and then leaped into the horizon where there appeared a dark hole which appeared to her as an opening to eternity. Slowly the line of souls became shorter until finally, it was her turn. She climbed up onto the great stone and prepared for her leap into the realm of endless night.

And just as she leaped, the face of her *tutuwahine*, her grandmother, appeared from the darkness of the hole.

"Go back, baby," spoke the loving voice of her grandmother. "It is nothing. Nothing. It is not your time. Go back. Go back."

Startled by her grandmother's warning, she pulled back from her leap, and fell away from the white rock. At that moment, she felt herself sitting up from her resting place, opening her eyes and looking about the parlor of her home on the island of Kauaʻi. She saw her relatives and friends gathered about the room, many of them screaming, fainting and praying. Looking down, she saw that she was sitting in a simple wooden coffin which had been prepared that day to carry her to her final resting place. It had been several hours since her body had turned cold, and the family in traditional fashion was burying her at midnight on the day of her death. Only now there would be no funeral.

Having been blessed with renewed life, this Hawaiian woman now was recognized as having great spiritual powers and insight among her family and friends. She possessed powerful healing abilities which she used only for the benefit of others. And having once been to the place where the souls of the dead leaped into the realm of mystery, she had conquered all fear of death.

The Haunted House of Waimea Valley

T he most famous haunted house on the North Shore of Oʻahu was once located on Kamehameha Highway at the entrance to Waimea Falls Park. An old wooden building surrounded by a large lawn and vegetation, in the early days it was known as the Honeymoon Cottage.

I had first learned of the reputation of the Honeymoon Cottage from a lovely woman named Jean Fowlds, with whom I had worked to publish her father's journal, *The Diary of a Blue-Nose Sea Captain.* Jean had lived in Hawaiʻi all of her life, her father having come to the islands as the captain of a sailing ship and then working as a railroad engineer at a sugar plantation on the Hamakua Coast. Although when I had met her she must have been over ninety years old, Jean was a spry, mentally alert and wonderfully warm person with beautiful blue eyes which literally twinkled when she spoke. She loved ghost stories and had signed up for my first "ghost bus tour" offered by Honolulu Community College senior citizen's program in 1984. Jean sat up front and absorbed every legend with enthusiasm.

Her experience at the haunted "Honeymoon Cottage" occurred when she and her new husband spent the days after their wedding on the North Shore. When they were sitting on the front porch at night, she explained, both of them heard the clatter of a horse-drawn wagon passing right in front of their house! Of course, the stagecoach which took passengers out to Waimea Valley had ceased operation many years before, Jean noted, but its ghostly memory still haunted the valley.

Inside the cottage, she continued, you could also hear a high-pitched call of what everyone knew were the spirits of the house. They called out through the walls, under the floor and down from the ceiling, vibrating the wooden frame of the building. It was a classic phantom sound, a "wooooooooo" that one would expect from an old horror film Jean Fowlds insisted that he and her husband had heard this ethereal being, and Jean was not a person to be challenged.

The structure was finally demolished in the mid-1980's after a lot of radio attention given to the "haunted house." When the property was cleared, an archaeologist informed me that he had been curious about it and was given permission to do a quick survey. In a few days they uncovered an older structure under the "Honeymoon Cottage"—an ancient site which was believed to be a fish shrine. As the research team was working on the site, several of them heard a faint "wooooooooo" rise from the earth. Following the sound, among the stones they located a small opening from which the eerie noise emanated. They then dropped a long rope into the hole to measure its depth. The rope extended over thirty feet before it reached bottom. Hauling it out, they noted that the bottom of the rope was drenching wet.

Evidently an old lava tube ran under the house into the nearby ocean at Waimea Bay. When the tide rose, the air in the but was forced out through the opening, which literally penetrated the earth into the walls of the "Honeymoon Cottage," emitting the unearthly call of the dead. The ghost had turned out to be a lava tube!

The news that the famous haunting in the house of Waimea Valley may have actually been produced by very natural phenomena was somewhat deflating. However, not far from the "Honeymoon Cottage" site, the archeologist found another older house site which he felt may have belonged to Manoheli'i, a relative of the Hawaiian historian Samuel Manaiakalani

Kamakau. If true, then this house was the site of an extraordinary event which took place in the 1820's, as recorded by Kamakau.

Manoheli'i's family *'aumakua* or guardian angel was *mano,* the shark. In the old days, it was customary for her family members who were buried upland, to have their bodies later taken to the sea. After her death, Manoheli'i's body was buried in a Christian fashion close to the back of her house in a hollow about seven feet deep. The coffin was an old-fashioned trough, and the body was wrapped in *tapa.* On the second night after her burial, it was said that a shark came and took away the corpse. In the morning, her family found a hole, 16 inches in circumference and seven feet deep, above her coffin. The wooden coffin itself had been splintered open, a gaping hole revealing that the trough was empty. No trace of Manoheli'i's body was ever found. Since the grave was about 20 feet above sea level, the shark would have had to swim out of the ocean, crawl to the burial site and dig up the corpse. The evidence it had done so was later found on the beach where a ridge cut by the shark's belly fins and side fins could be seen. The tapa in which Manoheli'i had been wrapped was scattered all over the beach.

A few years later in 1828, her brother Kuaila passed away. He was buried inside the house, dirt and *lauhala* mats being placed over his grave. The night of his burial, a shark opened a hole in the side of the home, dug up his body out of its grave and took Kuaila to the ocean. The sharks ensured that no bones of the family would be left on the land, but their remains always concealed in the sea.

The evidence that these events definitely took place at this site, or that the "Honeymoon Cottage" was somehow "haunted" by these ancient spirits will of course never be proven. In time the small, empty site will undergo many more future uses as posterity gradually forgets that at this place in the twentieth century a legend had once been born, then vanished. Yet whenever I pass that grass place at the hairpin turn of Waimea Bay, I can't help but reflect that even though many of the forms of life have changed with the coming of the *haole,* the foreigners, the *'aumakua* of the Native Hawaiian people still perform miracles in the islands imbued with the divine power of *mana.*

A Brief Encounter with Ka Huaka'i Po
The Nightmarchers

The spiritual power of Ka'ena Point is no allusion for anyone who has spent any time in this sacred place. The raw energy and beauty of this O'ahu district in the daytime is magically transformed in the evening as the universe of the Milky Way illuminates the heavens above with the dark, powerful cliffs of the Wai'anae mountains looming nearby. To know that this is a place for the spirits only adds to the sense that at Ka'ena, mortals can feel at times united with the unseen world.

As a *haole malihini* or newcomer who came nearly thirty years ago to live in Hawai'i, I had always assumed that the spiritual *mana* of the Islands was reserved for Native Hawaiians or other *keiki o ka 'aina,* children of the land who were open to the supernatural forces shaping their lives. What the "local" people saw or believed was outside my own cultural sensibility or understanding based upon our different upbringings. In other words, if you are reared in the cultural legends and beliefs of Hawai'i, you would be more naturally inclined to experience Hawai'i's ghosts and spirits. Ka'ena has helped me realize that these forces of supernatural presence are open to people of all ethnicities if they are willing to be open to them.

In 1992, I was camping with a group of students from the University of Hawai'i and the University of California in the

Ka'ena region at a place called Keawa'ula Bay—sometimes known as "Yokohama Bay." When the O'ahu Railway and Land Co. used to operate a passenger train around Ka'ena Point, they would sometimes let Japanese fisherman off at this place to fish. As a consequence, the area was nicknamed "Yokohama," an alias which has unfortunately erased the older and more proper native name to this beautiful white sand beach.

With the group was Keone Nunes, a Hawaiian cultural specialist and friend who was sharing some of the tales of the area with the students. He explained how the name Keawa'ula or "red harbor" was given to this bay. One interpretation suggests that the name referred to the *muhe'e* or cuttlefish which at times colored the bay red. Another version tells of how the great chief Kuali'i landed his canoe at this place after navigating the channel from Kaua'i. Set upon by marauders, he and his oarsmen fought them off, scores of bodies falling into the waters, the blood turning the bay red. He also spoke of a place near here called Ka-ho'iho'ina-Wakea, Wakea's turning-back place. As the spirit of the dead approached Ka'ena Point to go into the other world at *leina-a-ka-'uhane*, the soul's leaping place, they would be greeted by their *'aumakua* at Keawa'ula. If the guardian spirits did not think it was time for them to enter the spirit realm, they would be turned back to the land of the living.

At Keawa'ula was also a cave opened by the goddess Hi'iaka who was seeking water. This cave was once said to connect under the island to an extensive system of lava tubes which were like the catacombs of O'ahu. These caves were used as burial sites for the bones of the ancient *ali'i* or chiefs and were therefore considered *kapu* or sacred. The cave at Keawa'ula had collapsed in recent times, making entry into the burial areas impossible.

The stories continued into the early morning as the campfire ebbed and the wood supply shrank. The evening was cool with a stiff breeze blowing off the shore, and the students were huddled under blankets and sleeping bags. Since we had not even gotten to telling any of the ghost stories of the region, a couple of us volunteered to join Keone in fetching more firewood.

Using our flashlights, we walked off the beach and into the waist-high brush that extends to the base of the Wai'anae mountain about 150 yards away. Gathering up sticks of dry wood along the way, Keone led us to an area which was, unbeknownst to me, about fifty feet from the opening of Hiʻiaka's cave. Suddenly the air which had been very cool, changed temperature. While later many of the group claimed that the air was "warm," I felt the temperature rise to "hot," as if it were daytime in the beating heat of Kaʻena.

"Do you feel that?" Keone asked. "The change in temperature?"

All of us stopped dead in our tracks, noting the air get warmer. The breeze which had been blowing heavily also stopped in the place where we were standing. Yet another four feet beyond, the wind was indeed still blowing. The brush in that area was moving back and forth, while the tall grass where we stood was dead still.

"Listen!" added another student.

"What?" I asked.

"You can't hear anything."

Indeed, none of us could hear the wind or brush moving about only four feet away! The crickets and other night sounds which we had heard a moment before had suddenly stopped. The temperature seemed to me to be rising, as the eerie stillness continued in a ten foot circumference around us. Beyond the place where we huddled, the night was cool, windy and filled with sound.

"Interesting," said Keone Nunes in a low, nonchalant voice. "Very interesting."

"What's interesting?" I asked.

"Can you feel how different it is here?" His manner was now so calm that I assumed he was about to give us a natural history lesson.

"Yes, it is getting hot," I said. "What is it?"

"*Ka huakaʻi Po*," he answered.

"*Hua* what?" asked one of the University of California students who was unfamiliar with the Hawaiian language. Although I'm certainly not a speaker of the native tongue of Hawaiʻi, I knew what Keone meant. Nightmarchers.

"The cave of Hiʻiaka is right over there," Keone explained. "They seem to be approaching."

While the characteristics of nightmarchers in ancient Hawaiian belief vary depending on the source materials describing these spirit processions which march on specific nights of the month, all sources agree on one major point: don't get in their path, don't look at them, and don't collect firewood when they are marching your way.

Keone later laughingly remarked that since I am often referred to as a "ghostbuster," he was surprised that I was the first one to run out of this eerie place where natural signs indicated supernatural presence. However, I took note that he was right behind me. Some of the students from California perhaps didn't fully understand our concern to leave that place, but seeing the urgency in our demeanor, they followed right after.

As we moved away from the cave entrance, the air cooled, the breeze picked up and the sounds of the night returned. Back at the campfire, the other students had been anxiously waiting for the firewood and more stories. However, I told everyone that it was time to go to sleep. Tonight was not the night for ghost stories. Although some of the students complained that they wanted to get scared, it seemed to me at that moment a bit inappropriate to be discussing the spirits of the dead. We put the fire out as each student bundled themselves up for the evening.

"Do you think we ought to leave?" I asked Keone privately.

"It will be all right here," he answered. "We were walking over to their area and they were alerting us to stay away."

I lay back and looked up at the glorious heavens with billions of stars and galaxies surrounding a slight sliver of the moon. I felt relieved that the moon was not in the 27th lunar phase called Pokane, the night of Kane when the dead walk in processions. Yet I knew that whatever the date of the calendar, this night still belonged to the nightmarchers.

O ne evening in the 1980's, a Honolulu police officer who usually was stationed in the Kalihi district, found himself patrolling the grounds of the hotel located in Makaha Valley. A local *haole* who grew up in town, like a lot of other residents of Honolulu, he rarely went out to Wai'anae except as a teenager to surf at Makaha. Due to a shortage of officers in the Wai'anae area, he was now on temporary assignment working in an area he didn't know very well at all. As he passed by the hotel's golf-course, he looked down the valley toward Farrington Highway where he saw a blue light flashing on the roof of a slowly-moving car. Another officer was evidently pulling some driver over for speeding down on the main road through Wai'anae.

Following procedures, he got on his radio and called down to the officer.

"Does the officer need backup? Does the officer need backup?"

There was no answer.

He then tried calling the dispatch desk at the Wai'anae station. He reported to the officer on duty seeing a flashing blue light on a patrol car and asked if the policeman had called for any backup. The dispatch officer answered that no one had called in with an incident. However, perhaps he should drive down to Farrington Highway and give assistance if needed.

By the time he sped down to Farrington Highway, the car with the flashing blue light had accelerated, moving north out of Makaha Valley. He tried to close ranks with the speeding vehicle, but the other car was now accelerating even faster, the blue lights on the roof still brightly flashing. Whatever was happening, the officer reasoned, it was some type of emergency gauged by the speed they were traveling. His speedometer recorded that the car ahead was traveling over 70 miles per hour.

As they passed beyond Makaha, the road got narrower and more dangerous with dips and turns that were difficult to maneuver at half the speed. The speedometer now indicated that they were approaching 80 miles per hour as they passed Makua Valley. About 100 yards ahead the blue lights of the other patrol car flashed brilliantly in the pitch darkness of the clouded night.

Reaching down with one hand, he grabbed the microphone of the radio and started screaming into it.

"Will the officer respond? Will the officer respond?"

Still there was no response as they soared past Makua Valley.

"Damn it, will you respond? What in the hell is going on?"

The end of the road was not more than 200 yards away as they approached Ka'ena Point. Beyond the beach parking area, there was a four-wheel drive jeep road, but the boulders and potholes couldn't be driven at more than four or five miles per hour. At one point the road drops away altogether, making vehicular access to the tip of the island impossible. The other patrol car, he reasoned, would soon have to stop. He lifted his foot off the accelerator as he prepared to slow and finally brake. The other car, however, kept accelerating!

Stopping at Keawa'ula bay, the officer got out of his patrol car and watched as the other vehicle continued to drive out to Ka'ena Point. What in the hell was the idiot doing? He stood now yelling into the radio microphone.

"You are going to kill yourself! Stop! You'll kill yourself!"

Then, miraculously, the automobile with the flashing blue light on the roof actually accelerated! The officer estimated that the car was moving at a top speed of 150 to 175 miles per hour. The stream of blue light then hit Ka'ena Point with a huge explosion as if a bomb had gone off. A ball of blue fire radiated out from Ka'ena Point as the sky was brilliantly illuminated. In an instant, the light was then turned off, casting the entire region in absolute darkness. No stars were visible beyond the thick black mist of the now raining night.

"What in the hell am I doing here?" the officer said to no one in particular. In fact, there would have been no one to say it to. He was the only living soul on the beach.

Speeding from the area, his heart pounding, he finally raced back to Wai'anae where he found a couple of other police cars in the parking lot of McDonald's taking a short break. He was slightly trembling as he joined them for a cup of coffee, telling them what he had just experienced.

"You Kalihi boys need to learn something fast," they told him with a slight *kolohe* look in their eyes. "When you come out to Wai'anae, don't follow strange lights out to Ka'ena. That place belongs to the spirits of the dead."

After sharing that story with me, the officer unbuttoned the top few buttons of his shirt, showing a series of *kanji* or Chinese characters tattooed on his chest. He explained that he had converted to Buddhism a few years before the incident at Wai'anae and therefore consulted one of the priests concerning his encounter.

"The priest said that for my protection I should always have before me the words of the sutra, the holy words of Buddha. So I had a sutra tattooed onto my chest. As a policeman, I could use all the protection I can get."

A few years after this story was recorded, a couple of policemen informed me that there had been an officer killed a few years before in a car accident out on the highway going to Ka'ena. The strange blue lights flashing into the night, they agreed, could have very well been that tragic soul making his last journey to the place where spirits leave this world for the next.

Honu, A Family 'Aumakua

As Told by Cheryl Wilson

The *'aumakua*, or guardian angels can appear in many forms to their *'ohana* or family. These protective spirits can show themselves in the rainbow, mist or breeze. Depending upon the ancestral line of the family, they can appear as a shark, dog, chicken, lizard, owl, or even insects. Recently, one young Hawaiian man learned on three separate occasions that he and his family were protected by *honu,* the turtle.

As a child growing up in the 1960's, he had been told on several occasions by his grandfather that the *'aumakua* of his family was the turtle. He had been warned that he must never harm this animal when he was diving in the sea. If he was ever in trouble, the turtle would be his protector.

The words of an old man speaking superstitious beliefs had little meaning to this hard-headed young man until the time he met a turtle face to face. He was diving one evening in the strong currents off of Sea Life Park at Makapu'u. Night diving was an exhilarating experience that he often enjoyed—everything in the water taking on a kind of surreal effect. The water was dark and cold and he noticed a very large rock nearby. All of a sudden, the rock drifted upwards, shaking him visibly. Since when did rocks move? he thought to himself. Upon closer inspection, he saw that the rock was actually a sea turtle. He had never seen one so large or so close before. The turtle brushed past him, catching his attention once more because of its sheer size. He thought about the advice of his grandfather and felt comforted that the creature had swum with him that night so peacefully.

The second meeting with the turtle took place a couple of months later. This time he was night diving in the waters of Wai'anae. Out of the corner of his eye, he observed a large shark enter the vicinity, a shark much larger than he was accustomed to seeing. He watched the animal warily, as the shark began circling him, round and round, although keeping its distance. From out of nowhere, a large shadow moved swiftly through the water, heading toward the diver. The shadow turned into a sea turtle that hovered within arm's length of the young man. The shark, which had shown great interest in this human, abruptly turned and left, disappearing into the ocean's depths. The turtle, keeping the young man company for a few minutes as if to ensure his safety, then submerged into the darkness of the surrounding waters.

The third and final encounter between turtle and man took place a few years later. It was a beautiful morning and the young man and a friend had gone diving in Maunaloa Bay at Hawai'i Kai. He had become distracted, searching for salt water fish and had obviously stayed under too long, for he noticed apprehensively that the air in his tanks was running low. He moved quickly through the water, but when he cleared the surface, his friend and the boat were nowhere to be seen. Had he been under that long, that his friend had possibly left him alone, to get help?

There was nothing to do but to swim for the shore, which was now miles away. The current was incredibly strong as was the weight of the air tanks, which he would not drop, and he found himself fighting them both. He began to panic and in his despair, he began to pray, calling out to his family members who had passed on, and to his ancestors, to anyone who would heed his cry for help.

Just as he was about to give up his exhausted struggle and succumb to the inviting waters, a large sea turtle appeared from beneath the water's surface and came close to him. He looked at this creature and immediately felt an overwhelming sense of complete peace. The turtle turned in the direction of the shore and the young man followed, knowing that he would lead him back to the safety of the land. The current, which had been noticeably strong, seemed to change suddenly. The water felt smooth and calm as he swam easily in the turtle's path, focusing on this creature that had become his lifeline, his savior.

They had covered some distance and the land was close now. The turtle veered off, heading back toward the ocean, leaving an extremely tired young man to swim the final few yards to the shore alone. The ocean seemed warm and inviting, a place where he now knew his family ancestors offered their love and very grateful protection.

The Pauahi Dome

A distinctive blue-and-white dome sat on the top of the lava-stone Pauahi Building on Punahou School campus for many years until the late 1950's, when it was decided to renovate the historic building. At that time the dome was removed for refurbishing, but with the rising costs of construction and the delays normal in any administrative procedure, the dome was never replaced. In time, the plans to restore it were set aside as drivers and pedestrians along Manoa Road forgot about the handsome dome with the school colors that once graced the roadway.

One of Honolulu's most historic campuses, established in 1841 as a school for the children of Protestant missionaries, Punahou has had a proud history intricately tied to Hawai'i. Many of its alumni have played key roles in the political, economic, social and cultural development of the Islands. The names of the buildings represent not only several well-known figures in missionary history, but several royal names such as the Pauahi building, named for Princess Bernice Pauahi Bishop, the last of the heirs to the Kamehameha lands and wife of the businessman-banker Charles Reed Bishop. After her death, her lands became the Bishop Estate with the proceeds being used to establish the Kamehameha Schools. A friend of many Punahou alumni, the Pauahi Building was named to honor this beloved Princess and benefactress of Hawaiian children.

In honor of the 150th anniversary of Punahou Schools, it was decided that in 1991 the dome would be restored to its rightful place on the top of the Pauahi Building. A fund-raising campaign raised the necessary moneys as the dome was finally refurbished, repainted and brought to the building for reinstallation. One of the faculty members, herself an alumni, who worked long and hard for the restoration of the dome was on hand the day that the installation was to take place. A large crane had been brought to the campus to hoist the dome onto the roof of the building as the crew went to work. However, on the morning of the day of installation, the sky darkened as fierce winds began to blow through Honolulu. The installation was postponed.

A new date was scheduled, but for the next ten days, heavy winds blew through Manoa preventing the replacement of the dome. Finally one of the workers told the faculty member in charge of the project that tomorrow they were going to replace the dome, whatever the weather. A double crew was enlisted and they were ready to fight the winds.

In the morning, the winds and dark rain clouds again threatened the project. The teacher was disappointed that the weather would again postpone the installation of the dome, but she was assured they were going through with it nonetheless. At the exact moment of dome was to be lifted, the wind suddenly died. Everywhere else in Manoa, the sky was dark and gloomy. Yet for the next 30 minutes, the sky remained open directly above the dome with a vivid rainbow appearing overhead. The dome was gleaming in the sunlight as it was safely put into place and then secured. Once the work was finished, the wind suddenly returned.

As the dome was being put into place, the school band was unexpectedly walking by with their instruments. The teacher asked them to play the school anthem and a few other Hawaiian songs as the dome was lowered into place. Everyone agreed it was a "chicken skin" event, the way in which the sky and rainbow, with Hawaiian music, graced the restoration of the Pauahi dome.

When the teacher returned later that day to her office, she was beaming with the successful completion of the project and how the natural elements had cooperated very nicely with the construction efforts. Resuming her scheduling for the week, she looked up at her Hawaiian history calendar to confirm some dates. The calendar had interesting historic dates marked for the various days of the week. When her eyes fell upon today's date, December 19, 1991, the hairs on the back of her neck rose. The day the Pauahi dome was restored happened to be the 110th birthday of Princess Bernice Pauahi Bishop.

VANISHED INTO SHADOWS

K ualakai is a beach located on the west side of the Island of O'ahu near Barber's Point. In ancient times this beach was part of the Kaupea Plains which was famous as a land inhabited by the *lapu* or restless dead. These were the spirits of people who had died tragically or had no family to care for or nourish them in the afterlife. Perhaps they had committed suicide or were the victims of murder. They may have been evil in this world, so that no living descendant fed their memory or honored their lives. Bound then to an existence of hunger and restlessness, the *lapu* could not go into the spirit realm but were doomed to dwell amongst the living. These friendless spirits who hunted moths and spiders to eat at Kaupea were sometimes called the *po'e 'uhane hauka'e*, the besmirched spirit people. Today this broad expanse of west O'ahu can be enjoyed during a leisurely ride on the Hawaiian Railway Society train which takes passengers through this developing area.

Modern stories are today told of the eerie occurrences which sometimes take place at Kaupea and the beach at Kualakai. Mary Kawena Pukui related an unusual incident which took place at Kualakai years ago when her cousin, aunt, and she were walking from Pu'uloa to Kalae-loa (Barber's Point) accompanied by their dog, Teto. The dog was the ancient Hawaiian breed of canine the size of a fox terrier with upright ears. As they walked along the shoreline at Kualakai, Teto for some mysterious reason suddenly fainted, falling to the beach in a deadly stillness.

Mrs. Pukui's aunt immediately sent her into the ocean to fetch sea water which she then sprinkled over the dog while saying out loud:

"*Mai hana ino wale 'oukou i ka holoholona a ke kaikamahine. Uoki ko 'oukou makemake ili'o.*" Do not harm the girl's dog. Stop your desire to have it.

Saying a prayer to her *'aumakua* for help, the aunt rubbed the body of Teto who revived quickly. The dog was as lively and frisky as it had been before the paralysis.

"Then it was that my aunt told me of the homeless ghosts," Mrs. Pukui wrote, "and declared that some of them must have wanted Teto that day because she was a real native dog, the kind that were roasted and eaten long before foreigners ever came to our shores."

If one travels today through the shore called Kualakai toward Barber's Point on a quiet, dark night, they may still hear the drumming, the chanting, or the singing of the restless spirits. In 1986 during the filming of a television show entitled "Haunted Hawai'i," I escorted Chuck Henry and his ABC television crew from Los Angeles to the Barber's Point Naval Station. With the permission of the authorities, we drove to the beach at Kualakai with a small contingent of military police. During the filming of a segment of the program on the beach, the police became very interested in the fact that this area was considered a home of the restless dead.

"Many of us have heard drumming, laughing and Hawaiian voices singing on the beach," an African-American female officer explained. She had come to Hawai'i from Texas and knew nothing of local ghosts or spirits. Yet she had herself heard the mysterious noises on the beach at Kualakai in the early morning before sunrise. A brief inspection revealed that the beach was absolutely empty of any human life.

One officer, she explained, had an even more dramatic encounter. One evening he was making a short inspection of the beach while his partner waited in their parked police vehicle. As he took a quick look up and down the shore, he suddenly heard someone whistling. Walking a short way down the beach, he found an older Hawaiian man sitting by himself, smoking his cigarette and whistling. He looked a bit ragged and homeless as if he was intending to make his home on the beach.

The officer approached the old man and asked if he was authorized to be on the base. Was he military personnel? The old man just smiled and said that he was only enjoying the night. Again the officer insisted to see some identification which would authorize him to be on the military base. The old, kindly gentleman took a drag on his cigarette and told the officer that he had no identification.

"Let's go back to my patrol car, sir," the officer said politely. The Hawaiian man was certainly cooperative, he thought, but being on the beach without permission was a violation of the rules. "We'll drive you back to the front gate."

The old fellow rose serenely and walked ahead of the officer back to the parked vehicle. As they walked into a short access road to the beach, the officer watched the old man about three feet in front of him smoking his cigarette. Beyond he saw his partner waiting in the parked military vehicle. The old man gently whistled as a passing cloud allowed the moonlight to intensify, darkening the shadows of the tall trees that lined the access road. The old Hawaiian man stepped into the shadow, his whistle fading as the red tip of the cigarette moved about like a small firefly in the pitch darkness. The whistling faded, the cigarette light dimmed and the shadow of the tree blended into the dark form of the old man. When the officer emerged from the other side of the shadow, there was no old Hawaiian man walking in front of him. He had simply vanished.

"Hey, what happened to that old Hawaiian guy," the puzzled guard asked his partner. "Did you see him running off anywhere?"

"What old Hawaiian guy?" the partner queried.

"The one I was walking up from the beach with," he explained excitedly. "He was right in front of me."

"What in the hell are you talking about," the partner said. "You were alone. There was no Hawaiian man walking with you."

The guard leaped into patrol car, backed out on the main road and sped away from the beach at Kualakai. After his story circulated among the other guards, they all made sure when they drove the shore of the restless ghosts, that their windows were all rolled up tight and their music blaring. For if you don't hear the whistling of the dead, then you don't have to answer.

THE UNKNOWN ROOMATE

E lizabeth Chambers was excited to be visiting Hawai'i for the first time during the summer of 1991. Not only would she be enjoying a Pacific paradise which she had only dreamt about, but she would be able to spend a lot of time with her best friend from high school who had moved to the Islands during her senior year. It had been four years since Elizabeth and Jane Elders had attended school together in Plainsfield, New Jersey and although they had tried to stay in touch, letters could not substitute for those late night one-on-one chats which in their younger days had kept them up into early morning.

Jane's parents had purchased a large condominium in Honolulu, located on the top floor of a Nu'uanu Valley high rise overlooking the old O'ahu Cemetery. The unit had three bedrooms, one of which had been converted into a small office and sewing room used by Jane and her mother. Elizabeth stayed with Jane in her room, sleeping on a comfortable Japanese *futon* or mattress which was laid out on the floor each evening. The girls stayed up into the late night, talking about college, friends and boyfriends just like they had done in high school.

On the fourth morning of her visit, Elizabeth had a strange experience in the Nu'uanu Valley condominium which she would never forget. She and Jane had been chatting late into the night, so that morning Elizabeth had overslept. Jet lag had finally caught up with her, in addition to all the sightseeing the girls had been doing. Jane and her parents had already gotten up, fixed breakfast and gone off to do morning chores. A short note on the floor next to the *futon* indicated that Jane would be returning about 11:00 a.m. so that the girls could go to Ala Moana beach.

After her shower, Elizabeth walked through the condominium to have a light breakfast in the kitchen area. As she passed the third bedroom, she glanced in, noticing that someone was in the room. Sitting on a comfortable rocking chair in the office/sewing room was a pretty Hawaiian woman in her mid-fifties, wearing a colorful *mu'umu'u,* and a distinctive straw hat adorned with a feather *lei.* It startled Elizabeth to see someone else in the apartment, but she greeted the woman who returned the salutation with a slight, kindly smile. They looked at each other briefly, and then Elizabeth walked on to the kitchen to prepare her breakfast. It was an awkward moment, but the young New Jersey girl didn't want to intrude on this woman who she assumed was the Elder's family friend.

Jane returned just after 11:00 a.m. to pick up Elizabeth just as promised. As they were packing their things for the beach, Elizabeth finally asked her friend about the Hawaiian woman sitting in the third bedroom.

"Oh, you saw the Hawaiian woman in the bedroom?"

"Yes, I did," Elizabeth answered. "I was a bit startled, since I had expected anyone else to be here. Who is she?"

"We don't know," Jane responded matter-of-factly. "She's been here since we moved in."

"Excuse me?"

"She doesn't seem to harm anyone. My mother and I have seen her. My father thinks we are either crazy or making it up. But we think she is a ghost."

Sure enough, there was no Hawaiian woman in the bedroom when Elizabeth went back to carefully search the room. There was no way she could have left the apartment without having been seen. Directly across the street was one of the oldest graveyards in Honolulu. Could it be possible that a spirit from that hallowed ground had taken up a silent residence at this modern condominium? Who the roommate is, why she occasionally visits the Elder's home or what her intentions may be are questions which to this day remain unknown.

Myles Bunda had a ghost story he wanted to tell me. However, he insisted that I hear the story at the place where it happened. So early that evening I drove over to his house on a narrow lane in the Kalihi-Palama section of Honolulu. Myles was sitting on the porch, a local Japanese-American, well-tanned fellow in his early forties who worked for the city government. I turned on my tape recorder, and in his straightforward, no-nonsense style, he told me his ghost story.

"I've lived in this same location for about forty years now and I've seen many people come and go. Some of the young folks go to college and when they get good jobs, they move out of this area into the more affluent areas of town. I was born here. I like it, so I'm never going to move.

"That house over yonder is inhabited by the Tokushige family. The one next it, in back, was the first house on the property. The old place was there when my parents first bought into this district. It's about fifty years old at least. Mrs. Tokushige died in that house during the Korean War. That was back in 1952 or so. Her two sons were in the army at the time. Papa Tokushige was off in some bar so tipsy he couldn't come home. He never came home at all. They were a strange couple. No one ever saw them leave the house together. Oh, he'd come back to get some more money about once a week. Sometimes we'd never see him for about two or three weeks. They say that he was bitter because the American government took all his Japanese bonds away from him during World War II. It amounted to about $15,000. I can't imagine him ever having saved that much, because he was just a poor Japanese worker. He owned that store at the entrance to this lane.

"So when Mrs. Tokushige died, there was nobody there to help her. She lay in the house for at least a week before a neighbor found the badly decomposed body. The police autopsy revealed that she must have fallen and broken her skull. She died without anyone attempting to save her.

"My wife and I have heard many strange things happening in that house. In fact, my wife wanted some of the bougainvillea plants that grow wild around that house. She went up to pick some and felt a cold, freezing breeze and got scared and ran back here. Some people have seen lights on in the house at night even though Hawaiian Electric disconnected the wires about ten years ago. Michael Tokushige, their son, was living there for about five years or so but couldn't stand it. He wouldn't say exactly what his reasons were but we assumed it's that old Japanese lady coming out.

"The house has been abandoned now for the past fifteen years. Nobody wants to live in it and they won't sell it. The house is under the name of the two sons and several brothers and sisters who live in Japan. To sell that land they have to receive the consent of everyone and the brothers and sisters in Japan want to keep the property.

"I remember many strange incidents occurring recently, one which stands out most notably was told to us by a girl and boy who live in this neighborhood. One night my wife got me up because our dogs were barking. Evidently a car drove into the Tokushige's property. I got up and looked out of the window to see whether or not it was one of the Tokushige family. From what I could see it wasn't. Somehow my wife and I couldn't get back to sleep so we turned on the television. About fifteen minutes later we heard some screaming so I quickly put on my robe and went outside to see what was the matter. This boy and girl came running out of the house, terrified. They said they saw an old lady in there wearing an old faded *kimono*. I told them to say out of that old house and go home. They don't live in this lane because otherwise they would have known the circumstances which involve that house. They are both really good kids, my wife says, but a little reckless.

"A few days later a couple of kids who live across the lane from us were looking and pointing at the house. It turned out they go to the same high school as that boy and girl who were spooked the other night. Evidently there had been more to the story than they were willing to tell me or my wife when they had been frightened. I learned the full story from their friends.

"It seemed that Marcia and Glenn thought that this house was abandoned and a good place where they could 'make out' without being interrupted or discovered. That one night which I saw them was their first and I would guessed their last venture into that house. They went there about 12:30 a.m. and were starting to fool around when Marcia felt a very cold draft hit her body. Glenn didn't feel it till a little later. Everything around them was pitch dark. They continued kissing for about five minutes or so when they heard soft muffled foot steps approach them. Glenn thought at first it might be some hippie or bum who used the house for shelter. So he turned on the flashlight he had brought along, shining it about him. Then the light fell upon something moving in the room.

"Standing directly above them an old, old woman wearing a faded *kimono*. She glared down at them, seemingly saying to get out of her house. Glenn grabbed Marcia and the two of them dashed out of the house. That's when my wife and I found them screaming in the front yard.

"These two are the only persons whom I 've ever spoken to who have confessed to actually seeing poor old Mrs. Tokushige. Michael Tokushige moved to Boston and never says anything about the five years that he stayed in the house by himself. Yesterday I saw some man from T.S. Fujii's demolition company inspecting the house. I guess they're going to tear it down finally."

I thanked Myles for his story and walked over to the dilapidated homestead allegedly haunted by the unhappy spirit of Mrs. Tokushige. Like many old cottages in Honolulu, it was worn with the memories of the living and the dead who once occupied its now lonely walls. Some parapsychologists have suggested that ghosts are like recordings of energy trapped within the confines of a space where great suffering or pain had taken place. If such is the case, then poor Mrs. Tokushige, dying horribly alone on the floor of this house, is but a hollow wisp of her living form trapped endlessly as a recorded message in a her ghostly *kimono* shroud.

HONOLULU'S BUSY DEAD

Ka-ua-nono-ula (rain-with-the red-rainbow), according to William D. Westervelt in his collection *Hawaiian Legends of Old Honolulu*, was a place in the old village of Honolulu which was the home of the *wailua*, or ghosts. They would gather in this area for their nightly games and sports. At the turn of the century, Westervelt identified the ghostly site as "under the shadows of the trees, near the present Hawaiian Board Mission rooms at the junction of Alakea and Merchant Streets." These ghosts made night at this intersection a source of dread to all people. Another haunted intersection in Honolulu acclaimed for the gathering of ghosts was at the corner of King Street and Nu'uanu Avenue.

Today of course, modern Honolulu has been built up over this place of the rain-with-the-red-rainbow. The legend of *wailua* inhabiting these areas has been long forgotten, but the presence of these spirits has not entirely ceased in this modern Pacific metropolis.

Near the intersection of Alakea and Merchant Streets is an older building which has been the site of many small uncanny encounters with the supernatural. A law firm which once was situated in this graceful structure from an earlier period in Honolulu history, used to send many of their new staff members on my "Ghosts of Old Honolulu" walking tour. I was told that not only was the tour a nice orientation to downtown, but the stories of hauntings in the area prepared the staff for some of the subtle poltergeists which they may experience while working for the firm.

One of the legal secretaries shared a frightening experience she had had one night in the office. She had been working late to type up some legal papers required early the next morning, when she had an uncomfortable feeling that she was not alone. Her five senses told her that she was the only one on the second floor of the building, but her sixth sense suggested that she was being watched. Feeling terribly uncomfortable, with "chicken skin" on the back of her neck, she decided to quit earlier than she had anticipated. Securing the office, she went out the front door when she stopped dead in her tracks. She heard something in the office, a woman's voice calling out.

The woman was calling the secretary's name!

Thinking that there must be someone else in the office playing some kind of prank on her, she turned on the lights and looked everywhere. Her search turned up no one. She had indeed been alone in the office.

A field engineer for the telephone company years later confirmed that he also believed that this building was haunted. He had been installing new lines in several offices during a period of time when the building was unleased and empty. This was his first time in this particular downtown building and he was told by some of the more senior men to take care of the second floor installation. Everyone else stayed downstairs working with the ground level offices. He was on his hands and knees, working on installing a line along the baseboard when a piercing scream filled the room. It was an unholy, terrible scream that sounded like a woman had just been murdered. The single scream lasted but a few moments, but the memory of it left an indelible mark on the memory of the telephone engineer.

What in the hell is going on? he thought to himself as he leaped to his feet, looking out the window of the building. He half-expected to see some poor lady being stabbed to death or strangled on the city street. Pedestrians and traffic moved about unaffected by the murderous scream. Running downstairs he looked around the ground floor, but found everyone busy with their tasks as if nothing had just happened!

"Did you just hear a woman scream?" he asked of one of the other men.

"You heard it, too?" the senior man answered.

"What do you mean heard it too?"

"A couple of us have heard a lady scream when we work on the second floor. Why do you think we insisted you go up there and not us?"

According to this informant, he had been told that years before a woman had been found dead in that room. An investigation revealed that the actual cause of death was unknown. While I have not been able to confirm or deny that such a strange death took place inside that building, the telephone engineer continues to be convinced that this woman must have died of fright from something she had seen. And her screams still haunt the building at the place where the *wailua* remain busy in downtown Honolulu.

THE FIRST GHOST STORY
A Promise Fulfilled

L ouis T. Grant succumbed to pneumonia at the age of 58 years on February 14, 1928 in Los Angeles, California. The husband of Sadie Grant and the father of five sons, Louis, Howard, Clinton, Clifford and Elmore, he had for many years worked as a lens grinder for optical companies in several eastern United States cities, finally settling into a large farm outside Richmond, Virginia. In 1921, lured by the boosterism coming out of Los Angeles, believing that greater economic opportunity awaited his sons in Southern California, Louis packed up his family for a transcontinental automobile trek to the West. Converting an old Ford into what was touted as the first "station wagon," the Grant family drove nearly two months through plains, deserts, cattle and sheep ranges, Native American reservations, undeveloped roads to finally arrive in California in an era before "Route 66." Two years later, the patriarch of the Grant family was dead.

The funeral took place at Forest Lawn in Pasadena, California, a huge urban graveyard which would be a pioneer in developing the "theme park" concept in cemeteries. The day was dreary as a light rain fell over Los Angeles. After the coffin was sealed in its final resting place, Sadie Grant and her sons returned to their rented bungalow in Hollywood to prepare for the first real family meal they would all take together since Louis had died. Louis had always promised Sadie that if he should die before her, he would try to give her a sign that he had survived death.

The supper was taken in the dining room of the small bungalow, Sadie Grant sitting at the head of the table while her boys filled either side of the long wooden dining table. The eldest son, Louis, sat in his customary place in the middle of the table, with his back to a large old painting of a scene from the signing of the Declaration of Independence. Clifford sat directly across from Louis with the other brothers on either side of the table. The meal was solemn as each of them was filled with sad memories of their husband and father who had been such a dominating force in each of their lives.

Suddenly the two family dogs who adored the departed patriarch began to whimper and lightly growl. They had been sitting in their usual place during dinner, on the floor under the table where they would wait for their little snacks dropped by the boys. Now they made a bee-line for the front door of the cottage, where they jumped up and down in circles, barking and making an excited commotion. This was precisely their same behavior whenever father had come home after a day of work! The door to the house never moved. There was no vision of an apparition or translucent cloud. Yet everyone in the family knew that those dogs were joyously happy because they could see Louis coming back home.

The dogs excitedly followed the unseen father into the dining room, jumping up on their invisible owner as he evidently came to stand directly behind his eldest son and namesake. Clifford was sitting directly across from his brother Louis when the hair on the boy's head and arms suddenly stood directly up as if an electrical shock had gone through his body. Later he would explain that at that moment, with the dogs barking all around him, he had felt two very solid hands come to rest lovingly on his shoulders. The oldest son had received his departed father's blessing.

Then the entire Grant family watched dumbfounded as the large oil painting on the wall behind Louis came off the hooks on the wall, and gently fell to the floor with a thud. The heavy frame did not crash to the floor, Clifford would later insist, but almost seemed to move in slow motion. Someone had lifted that picture off its position on the wall and placed it on the floor. The wire backing was unbroken. The hooks on the wall were still secure. Yet the painting had come off the wall!

Sadie Grant later told her sons that many years before, their father had made her promise concerning their mutual interest in Spiritualism. He had told her that if he could, he would give her a definite "sign" that he had survived as a spirit beyond the grave. That evening, she firmly believed, the proof of an afterlife had been given by her husband.

Many years later on a early Sunday morning, Clifford Grant would tell his five year old son that ghost story as they sat about another family dining table. The boy had never heard any ghost stories before and was uncertain what his father meant by words such as death, spirit or afterlife. Yet his first ghost story fascinated him. He asked his father to tell him again and again. Like all good stories, it bore repeating. "I swear on a stack of Bibles," his father was fond of saying at the end of the tale, "this story is true." The young boy could not wait until breakfast was over so that he could tell all of his friends and anyone else who would listen about the spirit return of his grandfather that day in Los Angeles in 1928. As he dashed out of the house that sunny morning with a ghost story to share with Dickie, Jeffrey and Gary, he didn't know that he was running onto a long, unending pathway which would lead him through the strange world of chicken skin.

A Haunted Dormitory

In 1972 James Fujioka was an organizer for a special University of Hawai'i summer seminar which was hosted on the Manoa campus. Attendees from Hawai'i, the Pacific and Asia gathered for this important meeting of international educators who were expected to work and live together for one month. Because the University of Hawai'i was short of dormitory space, all of the attendees stayed at the old dormitory of a nearby private school which was within walking distance of the university.

The dormitory was a four-story structure divided into two wings per floor. There were small lounge areas on each floor and a main lobby adjacent to the office facilities located on the first floor. Dormitory rooms were quite pleasant and spacious, each one of them having a unique view of the University campus.

About one week prior to the arrival of the out-of-state attendees, James and a few of the other organizers decided to stay at the dormitory. Since this was James's first year with the program, he was anxious to hear from the others about the previous seminars. It was during these discussions that he learned from the other staff that the attendees in the past had reported "strange things going on" in the dormitory. In fact, some of them had gotten so scared, that they doubled up on the rooms, just so that they would have company.

James asked one of the girls if she could be more specific. What exactly had happened? She said that there was nothing terribly exciting going on—just "weird" things. For example, one night she left her light on her room before she went out. She locked the door to the room and no one else had access to her private space. However, when she later returned, the light was off. On another occasion, she left the light off. When she returned, all the lights were turned on in her dorm room.

Other odd little things happened. She always straightened up her room before she went off to the university seminars. But when she returned later than afternoon, her bed spread would be rumpled and thrown about. She'd be in her room reading, when the lights would suddenly start going on and off. When she left the windows closed in the morning, they would be opened later in the day. If she had left the louver windows closed before she went to sleep, in the morning when she awoke, they would all be open again.

The dormitory during the regular school year was a girl's residence hall. The master keys were distributed to the cleaning lady and to the seminar's administrative staff during the summer. If someone was playing a joke on the staff, then it would have been carried quite far. Others also mentioned how they had had these little strange occurrences going on in their dorm rooms.

James was impressed with the sincerity of the staff, but he was generally a skeptic when it came to ghostly matters. He had never seen a poltergeist or phantom, and did not expect to in his lifetime. When he took up residence in the old building, he was unnerved by any thought of lights switching on and off, windows opening by themselves or any other thing going "bump in the night."

About a week after the seminar started, James was watching the Johnny Carson show on his small portable television. His radio on a nearby shelf was turned off. He lowered the volume on the television and watched with his eyes half-closed as Johnny interviewed one of his guests. In no time at all, James fell asleep with the television still playing.

He was in a deep sleep when something jerked him suddenly back into reality. His television and radio were blaring with the volume turned all the way up! It was about 2:00 a.m. and both appliances were vibrating from the noise blasting through the dormitory. Before he could get up to turn them both off, he then heard a strange loud clicking sound from the side of the room. Turning to look at the windows of his dorm, he was frozen in fear.

The curtain which had been closed over his window was slowly moving on the metal rod, being pulled back by some invisible force. There was no wind that night outside or in the room. Yet the curtain distinctly moved, jerking along the rod and emitting that strange metallic sound. It was obvious that something either playful or sinister was trying to scare him. It was working. Wide-eyed in amazement and frozen in fear, James Fujioka experienced the most subtle of poltergeists as his closed-mind was pried open with a crowbar from the depths of hell.

A Haunting at Barber's Point

The conference was on "Death and Dying" and I had been invited to share some tales of Hawai'i's supernatural traditions at an afternoon workshop entitled "The Life After Death: Island Ghost Stories." The lecture hall at Leeward Community College was nicely filled with people from all walks of life who shared a common desire to know whether or not there was indeed an afterlife. Raymond Moody had recently published his work *Life After Life,* and the discussion naturally drifted into the direction of "near death experiences." Several individuals who claimed to have seen the ascending spirits of their loved ones soon after death also shared their visions.

As I was leaving the campus, a young *haole* man with closely-cropped hair which I perhaps unfairly assumed was a military cut, approached me in the parking lot. He introduced himself as Coast Guard Ensign William French, stationed at Barber's Point Air Station. Having read the announcement concerning my workshop at the college conference, at Leeward Community College, he made the effort to attend because he was very curious about Island ghost stories. He had only been in Hawai'i for less than two years, but he had had an experience which turned him into a firm believer in the ability of spirits to manifest themselves.

About a year ago, he continued at my urging, he had been assigned to shore patrol at Barber's Point. His responsibility was to cruise along the coastline, monitoring beach activities and making sure that all persons were authorized military personnel. Since there were a few military beach facilities that offered excellent camping grounds as well as some nice places for shoreline fishing, it was not uncommon for civilians to sometimes sneak into the area in the evening from nearby state beaches.

One night at about 11:30 P.M. while he was making his usual rounds of the base, he pulled into a beach parking area, surprised to see a yellow Volkswagen parked near a thicket of trees. He hadn't seen the VW bug during his first cruise of the area, so he pulled up directly behind it with his headlights shining right into the back window. Usually if it was a couple making out in the car, the headlights would pop their heads up like jack-in-the-boxes. No heads popped up.

Taking his flashlight, he walked up the back bumper of the VW to check for military decals. There were none. He then stepped around to the driver's side of the car and examined the front seat with his flashlight. Nobody was sitting behind the wheel. He examined the passenger's seat, but that too was empty. The back seat, from what he could see through the side window, was also empty. Someone had evidently parked the car and walked off to the beach. However, they had left the driver's car door unlocked, which he now opened to check for registration.

"Who is it?"

The female voice from the back seat made his heart miss a beat.

Jumping back, he was startled to see a young woman getting up from the floor in the back. He shined the light directly into her face as she got up, pulling an old military jacket that she had been using as a blanket up over her eyes.

"Your light hurts my eyes," she pleaded with him.

"Let's get out of there, ma'am," he ordered, swinging the VW door fully open and stepping back from the car. He took the light out of her eyes but kept it on her body as she pushed the driver's seat forward and stepped out of the automobile.

He described her as a diminutive Filipino woman in her mid-twenties with black, shoulder-length curly hair and dark, sultry eyes. An extremely attractive young female in a simple cotton print dress with a floral design, she clutched the army coat to her chest and rubbed her eyes with a wide yawn. Ensign French realized that he had evidently awakened her from her slumber on the floor of the car.

"What are you doing out here, ma'am?" he inquired.

"Resting. Am I doing something wrong?" She slightly smiled at Ensign French who, now relaxed, smiled back.

"Are you a military dependent, ma'am? I don't see stickers on your car. How did you get in?"

"I just drove in. Is there a problem?"

How had she gotten past the guard booth? he thought to himself. He'd have to give the guys out there a good scolding for letting a yellow Volkswagen drive right past them.

"Only authorized military personnel are allowed down here at the beach, ma'am. I'm sorry, but you'll have to leave. Get in your car and I'll escort you to the front gate."

Again the young Filipino woman yawned and stretched her arms out wide. Slightly shivering, he finally put the army coat over her shoulders. It had belonged to a large man so it seemed to swallow her tiny form.

"I'm so tired," she then said to Ensign French. "Do mind if I stay here a little while? I need to sleep." She again yawned.

Feeling a little sympathetic that she was perhaps too tired to drive her VW, but concerned that she was violating base rules, he trusted her enough to compromise.

"I have to first go up to the end of the road and check the other beach area," he explained to her. "That will take me about fifteen minutes. Why don't you wake yourself up and I'll be back to escort you out to the front gate, okay?"

"Thank you," she said, getting into the front seat.

"Now don't leave until I come back, okay?" he ordered her as he got back into his patrol car. She agreed to wait as he drove up the beach road, secured the area, and about twenty minutes later returned to the place where the yellow Volkswagen had been parked. Unfortunately, the young girl had not waited for him but had decided to drive off. Ten minutes later he sped up to the guard booth at the front entrance to ask the men whether or not the Volkswagen had left the base. One of the senior officers who had been stationed at Barber's Point for several years, grinned and shook his head.

"A yellow VW?"

"Yeah," Ensign French answered. "That's the one. Did it just come through here?"

"Filipino girl laying on the back seat floor? Army coat over her head?"

"Hey, how did you know?"

"What do you guys do, get together to work this stuff out?"

"What are you talking about? Work what stuff out? Did you or didn't you see that yellow VW?"

"Come with me," ordered the senior man. They got into his patrol car and drove back out to the beach. Ensign French showed the other man the place where he had seen the car and young Filipino woman. They got out with flashlights and examined the exact ground where the VW had been parked.

"Okay," said the senior man. "Show me the car tracks of a VW."

"Sure," answered Ensign French. "They should be right here. Hey, wait a minute!"

The tracks of his patrol car were clearly visible in the ground where he had parked behind the yellow Volkswagen. But there were no tire tracks of any other car in the area where a little over 30 minutes earlier the VW had been parked.

"What in the hell is going on?" he asked the senior man.

"You tell me," he answered. "Every time I get a new man like you on the shore patrol, they come in with that same cockamamie story. One of the other guys gave it to you and told you to pull my leg, right?"

"What are you talking about? I swear I saw that yellow Volkswagen with the Filipino girl inside!"

"Sure. So where are the tire tracks?"

Since that time forward, Ensign French explained, he's had a difficult time telling the story to others because it sounds so ridiculous. They laugh and make jokes about the ghostly VW. Is there a heaven for old cars? What were you smoking on duty? But he is absolutely certain that he saw what he is now convinced was a spirit vision.

"Do you know who the girl was?" I asked.

"Yes, I found out from the senior man that night. And I've confirmed that what he told me was absolutely true."

In 1965 a Coast Guard officer suspected that his local Filipino wife was cheating on him when she began to wane in her affections. Although she was actually innocent of any indiscretions, her husband was so jealous that one night he followed her when she went out with her girlfriend who owned a yellow Volkswagen. The two of them drove up to a house in Waipahu and parked. Believing that his wife was using her girlfriend as a cover to have a romantic rendezvous, he confronted the two of them, thrust a .45 caliber automatic revolver into the side of his wife and drove off in the girlfriend's VW. The friend called the police, but by the time they arrived her car and its occupants were long gone.

The husband was waved onto the Barber's Point base by the guard at the front gate who instantly recognized his friend behind the wheel of the VW. Even though the car had no military decals, the two men had known one another for years. The guard later told authorities that he had no reason to suspect foul play. He never really saw the man's wife in the front seat or any weapon.

The details of what happened later could only be told by the husband. At his trial he confessed that he had used the gun only to intimidate her, to make her confess to her infidelity. The gun accidentally fired as he waved it about threateningly. His lawyers asked that the charges be therefore reduced to manslaughter for he never intended to really murder his wife.

However, the prosecution prevailed on the charges of murder in the first degree. If it had truly been an accident, they argued, there would have been no reason for him to have pumped four bullets at close range into the face of his once beautiful wife. Even the jury was not allowed to see the autopsy photograph. What four .45 slugs at close range could do to a human face is best left only to the imagination.

The husband must have felt some remorse immediately after the murder. For when he was finished with his senseless act of rage, he covered what was left of his wife's face in an old khaki army jacket he had found in the back seat of the yellow Volkswagen. Then, almost lovingly, he placed her on the back floor, as if she were being put to bed for a long, eternal night of sleep on a lonely O'ahu beach.

Later that evening Ensign French accompanied me to the place at Barber's Point where he had found the phantom yellow Volkswagen. It was about 10 P.M. and the beach was desolate, the evening oppressively still with dark, threatening clouds obscuring a quarter moon. We walked silently down to the beach as if waiting—no, yearning—for something to happen. After so many years searching, the ghosthunter never fully loses the fear of the unseen, but there is always an overweening desire for some small manifestation to suddenly take place, the veil to be briefly lifted. No such revelation occurred that night, the haunted place concealing its secrets. Yet just as we were leaving, was it my imagination or wishful thinking that I felt a rush of cold air that swept through the parking area? My flesh tingled as I forced out of my mind the horror caused not by the dead, but the living.

THE PICTURE BRIDE'S STORY

No collection of favorite ghost stories of Hawai'i would be complete without retelling the "*obake*" story which I heard from a *issei* or first generation immigrant who had come to Hawai'i in 1920 as a "picture bride." Although this tale was incorporated into "Out of the Sea at Mokuleia," published in *Obake: Ghost Stories of Hawai'i* in 1994, I noted at that time that certain aspects of the story had been fictionalized and changed. The actual place where the strange incidents took place was moved in that retelling for a variety of reasons involving anonymity. I also at that time censored a bit of the story which I felt was perhaps a bit too risqué for readers of younger age. However, to preserve its original form, the full truth should be recorded about a modern encounter with a *mo'o wahine* or supernatural lizard woman at Mokapu Peninsula in Kane'ohe Bay on the windward side of O'ahu.

The daughter of the "picture bride" had first called me in 1986, inquiring if I would be interested in collecting the "*obake*" story which her mother had been telling for many years to several generations of family members. She had heard I was the "*obake* man*" of Hawai'i and thought that I would be impressed with the uncanny tale which her mother was willing to share. The date and time for the interview was set at their home in Kaimuki.

Following a delightful Japanese meal for lunch, we moved into the living room where I had set up my tape recorder and microphone. The elderly Japanese storyteller was at that time 92 years old, yet looked at least 15 years younger. She was spry, strong of voice and ebullient in her mood during the narration. The "picture bride" delighted in her opportunity to pass this story on to me for retelling so that the tale would stay alive through the generations.

During our lunch together, she had spoken to me in a very understandable pidgin English. However, just as soon as I turned on the recorder, she began her ghost story in Japanese. I was instantly lost and interrupted her apologetically.

"*Sumimasen,*" I said in halting Japanese, turning off the recorder. "*Nihongo ga wakarimasen.*" I did not speak or understand the Japanese language.

"*So desu ne?*" she said looking puzzled. "You *obake* man, and you no talk Japanee?"

I looked at her daughter very plaintively. Embarrassed at my language deficiency, I explained that I was like many Americans monolingual. Perhaps she could tell the story in pidgin English?

"No," her daughter explained. "Mama doesn't speak English that well to tell the full story. But don't worry, I'll translate her tale for you."

Reassured that at least I would hear the story second-hand through an interpreter, I pushed down the buttons on the recorder and sat back to hear a fascinating tale old Hawai'i from another time and place.

In 1920, she left Tokyo, Japan to come to Hawai'i as a "picture bride." She had never met her new husband except through their exchange of letters and pictures through an intermediary "marriage broker" selected by her parents. Frightened as she was to come to these distant islands to marry a man whom she had never met, she was relieved to find that he was a thoughtful, industrious man who treated her with kindness. He worked as a "shotgun guard" for the Waialua Sugar Plantation. When the shipment of "pay day" money was sent out once a month to the Bank of Hawaii at the plantation, he would accompany the driver as a guard, holding his shotgun in his lap and an ammunition belt strapped on across his chest. Today the old Bank of Hawaii building has been converted into a popular local bar, the old former bank vault still standing in the lot next door.

One of her new husband's passions was fishing, a sport he engaged in every weekend with his friends from the plantation. They would pack up an old truck and drive to all parts of O'ahu. While his new wife would always be invited along for these fishing expeditions, her chore was to cook the food for all of them while they went out setting their lines and nets. Since she was the only wife among the group of friends, she usually did this task alone at a campsite set up near the truck.

While they had many favorite places to go fishing, on one evening they explored a new area on the windward side of O'ahu. She interrupted her story to explain to me that she wasn't sure of the name of the place they were fishing, but she could locate it on a map. Her daughter brought out the map of O'ahu from the phone book and the "picture bride" instantly put her finger on the peninsula called Mokapu. While today that area is a part of the Kane'ohe Marine Corp base, in the 1920's people could fish in that area undisturbed by military authorities.

After finding a convenient place to park their truck, a campsite was set-up as the men spread out along the shoreline to cast their nets. The woman was left alone at the truck on a peaceful, quiet night at Mokapu. The campfire glowed as she steamed the rice in the illumination of a large kerosene lamp.

At about 11:00 p.m. she suddenly heard the voices of Hawaiians talking about 200 feet behind her in a thicket of brush. Not a sound or sight had come from that place a moment before, but as she turned to look in the direction of the voices, she now saw a dozen flickering firelights. Evidently a large group of Hawaiian fishermen, she thought, had also made camp in this area.

"Ah," she explained to me in Japanese, "I felt so safe being there with all those people! I was not alone on the beach!"

A few minutes later she looked down to the beach and saw that one of the fisherman was approaching the camp. Only on closer inspection she saw that it wasn't one of her husband's Japanese friends—it was evidently one of the Hawaiian fishermen from the camp behind her. As he walked steadily up the beach in a deliberate, calm manner, she noticed that he seemed to be naked except for a loincloth across his waist. She said that he stood maybe seven feet tall and his chest was massive and muscular. He was dragging a fishing net up from the beach behind him.

Having come to know in her short stay in the Islands that the Hawaiian people were very friendly, she wanted to call out to him in his native language. At this point in the story, she started replicating the call she had used many years before, crying out "Aroha! Aroha!" several times. I noted her "rolling r's" as a matter-of-fact, not intending to make fun of her. She admitted she may have had a difficult time making herself understood to the Hawaiian man since he kept walking on without responding to her call. So she decided to use English.

"Herro!" she said with the same distinctive Japanese accent. "Herro!"

The Hawaiian fisherman evidently now understood her because he stopped. In the darkness of the night she couldn't see his face at all, but he seemed to turn his head in her direction. He was only about 50 feet away from her as she decided to move closer to him.

"Herro!" she called again. Still he never answered her as she grabbed the lantern and walked over toward him. She held the kerosene light up as high as she could so she could see his face. His giant form towered over her as she approached closer, still politely trying to talk with him.

"Herro?" she again politely said. She was now looking up, directly into his face. His lips never moved. No words were ever emitted from the giant man. But he spoke to her very clearly with his eyes.

GET OUT OF HERE! the angry gaze told her. GET AWAY FROM ME! YOU DON'T BELONG HERE!

Her heart fluttered as she dropped the lantern and ran back to the camp. Hawaiians were usually so very friendly to us Japanese, she thought to herself. But this man is cruel and nasty. She decided she didn't deserve that kind of treatment as she was determined to give him the worse "stink-eye" she could muster. Scrunching up her face in a nasty glare, she turned holding up the lantern in front of her and shot him a look that could kill.

In the full illumination of the lantern, however, she saw something which turned the "stink eye" to a look of terror. She saw that the Hawaiian man had absolutely no feet! At the kneecaps, his legs faded to nothingness. Now impervious to the Japanese woman, this spirit resumed its steady movement as it floated to the campfires where the voices of Hawaiian people suddenly vanished. As the man passed each light, the fires went out one at a time until the last flickering flame died as if someone had blown it out like a candle. At that instant, the giant Hawaiian man with no feet vanished into the blackness of the evening.

"OBAKE!" she started screaming to the beach where the Japanese fisherman were busy pulling in their nets filled with fish. "OBAKE! OBAKE!"

Her husband ran up to her asking what she meant. What *obake?*

"No feet! No feet!" she answered hysterically. "*Hinotama! Hinotama!*" Fireballs, she explained, pointing in the direction of the campfires that had vanished. "Go look! Go look!" his wife insisted as the "shotgun driver" studied the dark, empty beach area behind them at a safe distance.

"*Obake!*" he finally said in a mocking tone. "Bursheeto, *obake.*"

"No bursheeto," she insisted. "*Obake!*"

In the entire story, she actually only spoke two English words: "herro" and "bursheeto" indicating that this salutation and descriptive term must have been the earliest two English words that new immigrants found necessary for their adaptation to the Hawaiian islands!

At her insistence, the husband finally went over to search the area with the lantern. He came back 10 minutes later, very excited and nervous.

"No bursheeto," he told her. The area where she saw the lights was an old Hawaiian graveyard.

On a few occasions I have been told by contemporary military personnel that there is actually no graveyard at Mokapu Peninsula as described by the "picture bride" in this tale. However, a recently-published history of the military base on the peninsula indicates that indeed there had been an old graveyard at Mokapu in the days before World War II. The base had been expanded in preparation for the predicted Pacific war and the bodies and markers had been removed. The "picture bride" and her husband had indeed been at this old sacred site of Hawaiian burials.

In a minute all of the men were called up from the shoreline except one man who was nowhere to be found. The husband told the youngest man to go fetch his friend, but he refused being frightened by all the talk of *obake.* Since no one, including the husband, was willing to go alone, they decided that all of them would go up the beach together to look for the missing fisherman.

Finally, at the very tip of the peninsula the man was found lying on his back unconscious, spread eagled on the sand. His shirt had been ripped off of him, baring his naked chest. Lowering the lantern over his face and chest, they saw something horrible.

At this point in the story, she lowered her voice as she recalled the fear that had run through her body that night at Mokapu. She spoke only two words which I understood without translation.

"*Midori desu,*" she said in deep seriousness. The skin of his face and chest had turned from the color of human flesh to a vivid green.

At first they all thought that he was dead, but when her husband put his hand on the poor man's neck, he shook his head.

"No *make!*" he said with hope. The man was not dead. They picked him up and carried him to the truck. His skin had returned to normal color as they rushed him to a hospital in Kaneʻohe. Although confined for a couple of days with a high fever, he completely recovered.

Later the "picture bride" asked the man what had happened to him? Why was he so far away from the other men? Why was his skin green?

He told the woman that when he heard her cries of "*obake*" from up the beach, he became frightened. It was dark and he had wandered far away from the other men. He immediately began to haul in his nets when he suddenly caught a huge fish. Pulling in the net, he was surprised to learn that he hadn't

caught a fish at all! A young, naked Hawaiian woman was all tangled up in the next as he dragged her to shore.

Apologizing profusely to the young woman, he helped her out of the net. He had evidently caught her by accident while she had been swimming in the night waters. As she finally stepped out of the netting, she smiled at this young Japanese man in a highly suggestive manner, stepping toward him. He was totally dumbfounded as she walked up toward him and then suddenly slapped him on the side of his head, knocking him to the beach. Leaping onto his back, she began to smack his *okole* as if she were riding a horse. He struggled to his feet as she laughed, playfully slapped his *okole* again and told him to carry her up the beach.

Piggy-back style, he carried her up the beach to the tip of the peninsula. Any time he slowed down or tired, she would laugh and slap his *okole* until finally he tumbled down, exhausted. His face and chest were soaking wet in his own sweat as she picked him up from the beach, lifted his body above her head and then slammed him down on his back to the beach!

At that point, the "picture bride" began saying something privately to her daughter in Japanese. They discussed it for a moment and then the daughter explained that her mother was a bit embarrassed.

"What is wrong?" I asked.

"Well," the daughter said shyly, "she wants to explain to you that...er...well, let's say the woman rode the man many ways that night, if you know what I mean."

The mother looked at me with a slight *kolohe* twinkle in her eye. Now it was my turn to be embarrassed as I nodded my understanding. She then continued her story.

After they finished their private business, the Hawaiian woman began to hungrily lick his face with her tongue which emerged long and sharp-pointed from her mouth. She was licking up the salt from his perspiration as if she was quenching her thirst on his flesh. He could see in the slight moonlight that she was gleefully smiling as her long tongue continued its strange feeding.

She then pulled away from him, grabbed his shirt with both hands and ripped it off of him, exposing his sweaty chest.

Looking down at him with an eternal hunger, the tongue in her mouth now extended longer, and longer and longer as it moved like a reptile from between her lips. Six inches long, then one foot, two feet, three feet. Finally, her tongue dangled four feet long as she licked the sweat from his chest and face. The world spun out of orbit as the waves crashed along the shore and darkness enveloped the Japanese man who passed into unconsciousness.

"That's the story," her daughter interjected. "She's *pau.*"

I sat on the couch a bit stunned. I had in no way expected that ending with the woman projecting a four-foot tongue. Ghost stories, after all, follow certain patterns. The footless Hawaiian man floating on the beach, the *hinotama* or fireballs that vanish in a graveyard, a supernatural woman coming out of the ocean—these are all motifs that confirm to the patterns of Hawai'i's supernatural traditions. Beautiful women with reptilian tongues sound more like bad "B" movie plots from American International than they did the lore of Hawai'i.

"Excuse me for asking," I then said, "but did your mom read this story? Or maybe make it up? Maybe it don't understand. This isn't a real story, is it?"

"*Honto desu,*" she answered directly, understanding my English. "True."

I returned puzzled to my office, convinced that I had had my leg pulled by one of the best storytellers I had ever heard. While I didn't doubt her sincerity, I was left with a bit of old folklore that just didn't fit any mold. That is, no mold of which I was aware through my personal collection of oral tales. But it was a few hours later that I realized that had actually read the story in a collection of old Hawaiian folklore. Thomas Thrum had a story concerning the *mo'o wahine* Kalamainu'u in one of his anthologies which I quickly reread. It was the tale of a supernatural lizard at Mokule'ia who seduced men, brought them to her cave and used them until they died. Most remarkably, in the tale told by Thrum, this Kalamainu'u possessed a tongue so long that she had the power to remove it from her mouth and use it as a surfboard which traditionally would have been over 12 feet long!

According to Samuel M. Kamakau in *Ka Poʻe Kahiko, The People of Old*, a definitive study of Hawaiian spiritual beliefs, a *moʻo* is described as a supernatural lizard, not the house or rock lizards known as the gecko. "The moʻo," Kamakau writes, "had extremely long and terrifying bodies, and they were often seen in ancient days at such places as Maunalua, Kawainui and Ihukoko at Ukoʻa." Their size could be anywhere from two to five fathoms in length and their skin was black as the night. Having supernatural powers, they could take any marvelous shape which they desired, including that of a human female.

I then researched the place name "Mokapu" and some of the history of the peninsula. The standard definition given in *Place Names of Hawaiʻi* by Mary Kawena Pukui, Samuel H. Elbert and Esther T. Moʻokini is "sacred place," a contraction of *moku* (place or district) and *kapu* (sacred). This name was given to the area because Kamehameha I and his chiefs met at the peninsula following his conquest of Oʻahu. However, other sources have suggested that a *moʻo* bathed in the waters of this peninsula, a female water spirit named Hauwahine. This is the *moʻo* which lived at Kawainui fishpond as described by Kamakau. Today, the ancient fishpond of Kawainui is a marsh at Kailua.

Adding to the spiritual *mana* of Mokapu, the peninsula once was marked by several Hawaiian *heiau* or temples some of which were destroyed in the late 1930's for the construction of concrete runways for the airbase. The place where the Japanese man was pounced upon by the mysterious woman is near the disappearing rock of Kuau which is called Pyramid Rock. It was known as a disappearing stone because sometimes it could not be seen, but would then reappear. It was believed that the stone also produced children, the newer stones being born to help protect the land at Mokapu from being washed away into the sea. Two stones called Ku and Hina were visible in the 1920's near Pyramid Rock. However, a man named George Moa threw these stones into the deep water so that they are not visible today. Moa went insane and died after his thoughtless deed.

After a recent storytelling session at Mokapu military base, I was approached by a young woman in the armed services who shared with me her own encounter near Pyramid Rock. She had taken her dogs running along the shore line in the early evening, just after sunset when they ran over a little sand dune, beyond her vision. Suddenly on the other side of the dune, she heard them begin to frantically bark, as if they were being attacked. She ran to their rescue to the top of the sandy knoll where she stopped dead in her tracks. Her two dogs were growling viciously at two huge white, glowing mists which hovered a few feet over the beach at the very tip of the peninsula. Although the sun had definitely set, these mists were illuminated in the still night, moving slowly toward the animals which turned and ran back to her jeep parked a few hundred feet up the beach. The mists then stopped moving, hovered a moment longer and then evaporated right in front of her shocked eyes.

When I listened to that short tale of an uncanny encounter at Mokapu, I once again pondered the marvelous way in which people who are newcomers to Hawai'i are still allowed the privilege to witness the forces of the supernatural in the Islands. Perhaps in some way my fondness for the tale of the "picture bride" lay in the pure innocence of the tale. For although this new immigrant had no prior knowledge of Hawaiian legends, ghostlore or *mo'o*, she and her companions had that quiet night on Mokapu peninsula stepped from this world, right into the living soul of Hawaiian mythology.

THE *MUJINA* OF 'EWA BEACH

C an an *obake* actually be "cute?" While this is not usually a
question which would concern most people, it certainly drew
the attention of one Japanese-American couple who lived in
a residential street in the 'Ewa Beach district. They told me how
one night at about 10:30 p.m. they were in their bedroom getting
ready to retire. As the husband was just drifting off to sleep, he
suddenly heard outside on their driveway a distinct sound.

"Kara karon, kara karon," he heard outside his bedroom
window. "Kara karon, kara karon." His wife woke up also,
confirming that the sounds were very real.

"Kara karon, kara karon."

They both agreed that the distinctive clacking was the sound
that old-fashioned Japanese wooden geta or sandals made on
cement. They had both watched enough Japanese *samurai*
movies to know that very special noise. Only in this case, the
geta were moving on their driveway outside their bedroom
window, approaching their garage!

What in the world would anyone be doing wearing wooden
geta in 'Ewa Beach?

The husband went to his bedroom window and looked out
on a very odd scene. A small, old Japanese woman in a red
kimono and holding a red umbrella was moving slowly down

their driveway. She was wearing wooden *geta* which were clacking on the cement as she took her little steps, her back slightly bent. Her snow-white hair was piled high up on her head in very neat coiffure fashion. The red umbrella was made out of paper and wooden sticks and was held slightly at an angle, casting a shadow across her face. She moved steadily down the driveway as she began to pass their bedroom window.

"Honey," the husband called, "come here! You gotta see this lady! She is so cute!"

The wife joined her husband at the window, gazing out at this strange figure of the red *kimono*-clad lady. As she passed their window, the old Japanese woman turned her head slightly, the shadow of the umbrella pulling away so that the couple could look directly into her face. Both their knees buckled as their flesh tingled with the sensation of a million tiny insects crawling across their skins.

The woman they were looking at had no eyes, no nose and no mouth. Instead of the features of a human face, she appeared to have the features of a smooth, white egg.

Horrified, they watched as this *obake* continued to pass their window and move into their garage. The red umbrella was visible above their parked car, but neither the husband or wife could see her body through the vehicle's windows. As the figure moved into the back of the garage, it vanished, never to exit.

The couple had very little sleep that night, wondering if they had just experienced some form of collective hallucination. Had the faceless woman really passed their window? The next morning, there was confirmation that their vision was not imaginary, but based in some form of reality.

The neighbors were in the front of their house with their son who was showing his parents exactly where he had had a strange encounter the night before. The couple listened as the young man insisted that he had seen a red *kimono*-clad old Japanese woman, holding a red umbrella, walk down their driveway. While he never looked at the woman's face to discover its featureless horror, he did confirm that there was a very solid figure walking past their bedroom window the night before.

THE FACELESS GHOST STILL HAUNTS
the Vanished Theater

In Japan, the faceless ghosts of tradition were known as *mujina*. These were not technically the spirits of the dead, but supernatural creatures who stalked the night. Sometimes they could almost be cute, appearing as *nopperabo*, formless blobs of flesh that were sometimes depicted by artists as almost comical monsters. For the couple of 'Ewa Beach, however, the cuteness or comedy of their neighborhood *obake* would always be tempered by the unforgettable shock they experienced when they looked directly into the faceless side of terror.

The first appearance of a faceless woman of Honolulu was at the old Waialae Drive-in once located in Kahala. A woman reported to the management that she had seen a lady without any facial features inside the women's restroom in 1959. Although the manager denied knowing anything about the haunting, everyone who ever went to the drive-in theater knew that next door to the grounds was an old graveyard. It must have been the spirits from the cemetery, the story was told and retold, who must have come to visit the ladies toilet! The popular journalist Bob Krauss did a special story on the incident in the Honolulu Advertiser, and the urban legend of this distinctive ghost was on its way into local history.

While the graveyard of Kahala is still located on Waialae Avenue, many other changes have come to the neighborhood. On one side of the cemetery, the favorite local diner "Jolly Rogers" has been torn down, soon to be replaced by a major restaurant. So too has the theater met the wrecking ball as the old drive-in grounds have been developed into both residential and commercial units. Like many of the neighborhoods in Honolulu, the older familiar landmarks of "places of the heart" are being replaced by new buildings, new businesses and new residents as each generation supersedes the other.

One wonders whether or not the spirits of the dead who remain in this world don't sometimes feel disoriented by all the physical changes taking place. Do the dead sometimes get lost in unfamiliar surroundings?

The faceless woman may indeed feel a bit homeless now that her famous toilet no longer exists. On December 6, 1996, two young men reported that they had been enjoying a feature film at a nearby theater complex located at a shopping mall. The movie finished at 10:30 p.m. and they hurried to the bus stop on Waialae Avenue to catch the last bus going into downtown Honolulu where they both lived. This bus stop is located directly in front of the old Kahala cemetery. There was no one at the stop except an older woman who sat on the cement bench. She was stooped over a large bag which she held in her lap. Her long gray hair was stringy and draped down over the side of her face. From her quiet demeanor, she almost seemed to be half-asleep.

The young men didn't want to disturb or intrude upon the lady, so instead of sitting on the bench, they sat on the ledge of a high wooden fence which conceals the graveyard beyond. Evidently for the peace and quiet of the resting dead, or the comfort of the pedestrians or bus passengers, the cemetery is concealed from streetview except for the front opening which is accessible to automobiles. The time passed as the boys talked story. The bus never came.

"Auntie," one of them said finally to the silent woman. "Auntie, excuse! Do you know what time the bus is coming?"

She didn't respond, but continued to rest on the bench.

"Auntie!" he now said louder, going over to her. "Did we miss the last bus? Is another one coming?"

The lady was evidently very hard of hearing. She gave no response to the young man. He walked over and stood next to you, bending down toward her so that he could be clearly heard.

"Excuse me, Auntie. What time is the bus coming?"

She never answered, but she looked up at the now stunned young man. For the lady on the bus stop had no eyes, no nose and no mouth.

He fled from the woman with all his might, running down Waialae Avenue back toward the shopping mall. He never made a sound, just turning and running with all of his might. He never looked back.

His friend sat on the ledge of the fence, wondering what was happening as he watched his friend run off to the mall. The elderly lady, he said, simply stood up, turned and walked back toward him, moving to the front opening of the cemetery. He took one look at her face and knew instantly what had made his buddy run off. Screaming, he followed his friend in beating a hasty retreat.

Had the faceless woman made a reappearance to her former haunted grounds, only to find that her restroom had been removed? What happens to a ghost without a haunt? Do these homeless phantoms seek out new accommodations?

A Phantom Hitchhiker at Salt Lake

In ancient times Pele came to the Hawaiian islands on a search for a home of fire. When she visited the Island of O'ahu, she dug several pits looking for her fires, leaving behind many empty craters. Thus she dug the craters of Pu'uowaina or Punchbowl, Kaimuki, and Leahi or Diamond Head. In one place where she dug, some of the viscid matter from her eyes dropped and formed a lake of salt. This area was called Alia-pa'akai or the salt pond. Today the area is better known as Salt Lake, a major Honolulu residential area with high-rises, homes, a golf course and only the tiniest remnant of the once famous salt pond.

A Hawaiian woman who lived in Salt Lake district in 1973 told me how one evening at about 10:00 p.m. she heard a knock on her door. When she looked through the doors' peephole, she saw an elderly, *kimono*-clad Japanese woman at least 90 years old standing peaceful on the porch. Her face was covered in wrinkles and her silky white hair was tied up on her head. She was holding a small stick over her shoulder to which was attached a small cloth bundle. This method of carrying one's personal belongings struck the Hawaiian woman as being very old-fashioned.

"Can I help you," the woman politely asked as she opened the door for the old *tutu*. The face of the Japanese lady smiled widely as she spoke in perfect English.

"May I have some water?"

The Hawaiian woman didn't hesitate for a minute, but excused herself and went to the kitchen to get this elderly Japanese woman her water. When she returned, the old lady was gone. There was no *kimono*-clad woman on the porch, on the walkway to her house or on the sidewalk. Being so old and fragile, the Hawaiian woman asked herself, how could that old *tutu* have moved so quickly out of sight?

She thought about that elderly Japanese woman for the next few days. Knowing every family on her street, she knew for certain that she wasn't a neighbor. The woman could have been visiting one of the other families. Out for an evening stroll, she could have become thirsty and needed the glass of water. But why didn't she wait for her drink? And how had she apparently vanished so quickly?

A few days later, one of her Japanese-American neighbors called her for some unusual advice. It seemed that her son who attended Moanalua High School had had a frightening experience coming home the other night. She wanted to know how to protect her boy using Hawaiian spiritual methods.

"What happened?" the Hawaiian woman asked.

The son told the following story. He had been returning home a few nights earlier to Salt Lake with a car load of his friends. It was about 11:30 p.m. as they drove a long, straight stretch of the road in the back entrance of the district when they saw an elderly Japanese woman in a *kimono* standing on the curb. As they approached her, she lowered a bundle of cloth that she held at the end of a stick, motioning the car to stop. While all of his friends told him to keep driving on, the son slowed his car down to give the old woman some assistance. Oddly, the engine died as he came to a complete stop.

"Can I help you?" he asked the woman.

"I need a ride," she answered in perfect English. He remarked that her face was remarkably wrinkled, as if she were 100 years old.

All of his friends now adamantly looked at him with a definite gesture of "NO!" But he had been reared to respect his elders and if this woman needed a ride, then she would get one.

"Sure. Why don't you get in back?"

His frightened friends looked at him as if he were crazy. A lonely road at night, a stalled car and an ancient old hag? Was he being *lolo* giving her a ride? The guys in the back seat slid out the other side of the door, made a lame excuse about preferring to walk home and let the woman have the seat to herself. His friend in the front seat joined his buddies on the walk home, leaving the driver and his unusual passenger alone.

"So where do you want to go?" he asked the Japanese woman as he tried to get the car going. The ignition cranked over, but the engine didn't start. His parents had just had the automobile tuned up!

"I don't know what's wrong," he explained to her. "Something is wrong with the engine." The sound of the ignition grinding continued as he pumped the gas pedal. Still the engine would not start.

"I'm sorry," he finally said, "but I'll have to call my parents. The car just won't start."

He turned around to explain this to the woman who had sat perfectly still in the back seat, not uttering a sound since she had gotten into the car. To his surprise, however, there was no woman in the back seat! The old lady had completely vanished! She was not only not in the car, but she was nowhere to be seen on that lonely Salt Lake road.

Testing the ignition again, the engine started up with no problem. He put the car into gear, hit the gas and nervously drove past his friends who were still walking home. When he later told his parents what had happened, they were a bit suspicious that the tale was a fabrication. However, his friends did verify the existence of the elderly Japanese woman. They decided to call the Hawaiian neighbor who perhaps could advise them on the best spiritual protection for their son.

After the Hawaiian woman had heard of the young man's encounter with the same Japanese woman on the same evening as her own visitation, she was convinced that Pele had come back to Salt Lake. For the goddess of the volcano, she explained to me, could take many body forms. She could appear as a woman of any race or age, wearing whatever clothes she wished. Pele had asked for the water; she had asked for a ride. She was testing the open-heartedness and *aloha* of the residents of the place that she had created from the tears of her eyes.

A professor of business at the University of Hawai'i approached me after I had given a lecture on supernatural Hawai'i to one of the most hostile audiences I had ever had the misfortune to address. A business club at the university had asked me to share ghost stories with the students at an opening meeting attended also by the faculty. While I am not judging the attitude of business people as being more materialistic than spiritual, the reception to the notion that spirits walked after death was not well received by those who need to balance both sides of the debits and assets ledger book.

So when this tall, bearded *haole* professor in an immaculate suit and tie approached me after the presentation, I was prepared for an assault upon my credentials or mental capabilities. Instead, I received one of the most direct, heart-felt and vivid first-hard accounts of the supernatural that I have ever heard.

"My wife and I were driving home late one evening to Hawaii Kai," he said to me, "when I slowed down to let a jaywalker cross the Kalanianaole Highway. As I neared the man, I saw that the jaywalker was nearly seven feet tall! He had no clothes on except for a white loincloth or Hawaiian *malo* about his waist. This strange man was totally oblivious to our automobile until he stepped directly in front of the headlights. I had come to a full stop, when this man suddenly turned to stare directly into our car. Both my wife and I were terribly startled, and we instinctively locked the doors and rolled up the windows.

"Then this huge, broad-shouldered and muscular Hawaiian," the professor continued, "walked toward the car. I thought he was going to highjack or assault us. However, the gaze of the giant was not threatening, but astonished. He walked up to the hood of the automobile, studied it in wonder as if inspecting such a modern vehicle for the first time. He then walked around to my wife's side of the car, leaned down and pressed his face and hands right up to the glass, peering in at her as if she were some strange alien.

"We watched him as he returned to the front of our car, turning his back to us. In the glare of the headlights, we were astonished to see the massive Hawaiian man dematerialize right before our eyes!"

This matter-of-fact expert in the material realities of our economic lives had been spiritually changed by his touch with Hawai'i's supernatural. Of course, he confessed, he would never tell any of his colleagues of his experience. He had a reputation to maintain. However, from that day forward, he confessed, he would no longer ridicule the tales he heard in Hawai'i, preferring to always maintain an open mind.

TERROR AT THE PALI TUNNEL

T aking pork over the Ko'olau mountains via the Pali Highway has long been recognized in Hawai'i as a serious breach of supernatural etiquette. The stories are countless of individuals who have had strange problems with their automobiles as a result of neglecting this very basic principle which may derive from a variety of different cultural or spiritual sources. When the first foreigners began to visit the Pali lookout in the nineteenth century, they noted a curious custom followed by Hawaiians attempting to traverse the dangerously steeply precipice. A London missionary William Ellis who visited the Pali in 1823 described two stone *ki'i* or images which where once located at the pass:

"Within a few yards of the upper edge of the pass, under the shade of surrounding bushes and trees, two rude and shapeless stone idols are fixed, one on each side of the path, which the natives call Akua no ka Pari, gods of the precipice; they are usually covered with pieces of white tapa, native cloth; and every native who passes by to the precipice, if he intends to descend, lays a green bough before these idols, encircles them with a garland of flowers, or wraps a piece of tapa around them, to render them propitious to his descent; all who ascend from the opposite side make a similar acknowledgment for the supposed protection of the deities, whom they imagine to preside over the fearful pass. This practice appears universal, for in our travels among the islands, we have seldom passed any steep or dangerous paths, at the commencement or termination of which we have not seen these images, with heaps of offerings lying before them."

The practice of making a small offering to the gods before attempting to pass over the Koʻolau mountains may have thus been the folklore custom which gave rise 100 years later to the modern notion that a traveler with pork would encounter car trouble trying to drive the Pali Highway. When the automobile stops with strange mechanical problems, the dispensing of a portion of the pork to the side of the road usually resolves the problem. Having fresh meat in your possession without making some kind of offering to the protective gods of the pass may account for the breakdown of the vehicle.

Another perhaps modern suggestion of the origin of the "pork over the Pali" folk custom relates to the legendary stories of Kamapuaʻa, the demi-god of Oʻahu and his tempestuous relationship with Pele, the goddess of the volcano. Following many intense and sometimes violent encounters between the two supernatural deities, an agreement was made that he would no longer visit the domain of Pele. Since Kamapuaʻa lives on the wet windward side of the island, and Pele on the dry, hot leeward side, the Koʻolau mountains serve as a barrier between the deities. By taking the body form of Kamapuaʻa over the Pali, then, the motorist has violated this ancient injunction.

One of the most terrifying tales which I have collected of a strange encounter taking pork on the Pali Highway was shared by a taxicab driver who in 1981 was waiting for a fare at the old Armed Forces Y.M.C.A. building located at Hotel and Richards Street in downtown Honolulu. It was still before midnight as he kept his dispatch radio on, scanning the various calls between the main office and the drivers carrying passengers around town.

Suddenly a piercing scream came over the radio. One of the female drivers who had a little earlier taken a late night bar-goer with too many cocktails to his Kailua home, was screeching into her microphone a desperate call for help. Her terrified voice sent chills down the taxicab driver who assumed instantly from her screams that she was being robbed or even possibly murdered. When her signal died, he called in to the main dispatcher to confirm that he had also heard the horrible screams. Indeed he had and had already alerted the police.

It seemed like an eternity before the female driver called back in to inform dispatch that she was all right but couldn't drive her cab. She was located just on the leeward side of the Pali tunnel in the Honolulu-bound lane. Could somebody come up to the highway and bring her back to the office? And someone would also have to bring her cab back in to town. She wouldn't go near the vehicle.

About one hour later, the very curious taxi driver was listening to an extraordinary tale told by the very shaken female driver who was now back safe and sound in the main office. Her hands were shaking as she took deep drags from her cigarette and sipped on her coffee from a Dixie paper cup.

Outside her taxicab was being parked by one of the drivers who had been taken out to the Pali tunnel to fetch the abandoned car.

"I had dropped off my fare in Kailua," she explained, "and was driving back to Honolulu. As I drove into the tunnel, I suddenly felt the air change in the cab. Like it got thick. Then something grabbed me from the back seat, grabbed my head like this."

She put a powerful grip on the neck of one of the other drivers and shoved him forward, demonstrating how she had been assaulted.

"I was shoved right up to the steering wheel so violently, that I almost lost control of the car. I thought somebody had gotten into the back seat and was trying to rob me. I reached down and got the mike to call for help. I was screaming like hell.

"Then this thing shoved my foot down to the gas pedal! I shot out of the tunnel going 80 or 90 miles per hour! I never saw nothing on my foot, but my foot pressed down hard on the gas!"

A shiver went down the back of everyone in the room as they imagined being held in the powerful vise of a hand, pressed against the steering wheel as an invisible force accelerated the car. Unbelievable.

"I flew out of that tunnel heading for the side of the railing. I knew I was going to die. Then that thing let go of me. Just like that, it let go of me."

She had come to a skidding stop at the side of the road and fled from the haunted vehicle. As she expected, there was absolutely no one in the back seat of her cab. After a few minutes of calming herself down, she finally had mustered the courage to call into the main office for help. Other than that, she wouldn't go near the vehicle again.

"Whatever was in that car," she concluded with conviction, "could have killed me. I thank God it let me go."

By that time the driver who had brought her taxicab back to town came into the office with a small paper sack which he put on the table in front of the driver.

"Here's your dinner," he said. "You left it in the car."

"That's not mine," she answered. "Where did you find that?"

"In the back seat. I figured it was yours."

Her drunken passenger had evidently picked up a sandwich before his ride home. When he tumbled out of the car at his Kailua home, he had forgotten it in the back seat. Inspecting the package, the drivers found that he had a fondness for barbecue pork.

"I'll kill that guy," she muttered, realizing now what had been the cause of her supernatural distress. "I was driving with pork over the Pali!"

A Brief Encounter at the Pali

The Japanese television company had come to Hawai'i to do a special "*obake* season" program for a popular series based in Tokyo. The summer time is usually a period when ghost stories are very popular in Japan, so the producer of the series decided that a Hawaiian connection would be very interesting to the viewers. The format of the program was based on a simple quiz show premise: popular Japanese television personalities would be asked a question about supernatural beliefs in Hawai'i through a video clip filmed in the Islands and they would then guess the answer before a live audience. Due to my reputation as the "*obake* man," I was invited to be the host of the questions video taped at various sites around O'ahu and the Big Island.

I was a bit leery of the format of the program which could be quite silly in terms of the various answers the personalities could give to the questions. I had seen other Japanese television shows which were sometimes a bit insensitive to the host cultures which they were exploring. So I insisted that the places which we went to for the filming were not related to Hawaiian sacred sites—no temples, burials or other spiritual places. We would concentrate on urban legends such as the faceless ghost or haunted dormitories.

The producer had however done his homework. A bright young man in his mid-thirties, he had an avant garde style which reflected his international experiences. He had heard about the "pork over the Pali" stories and insisted that we include a late night visit to the lookout on our tour. With a little hesitancy I agreed under the condition that the presentation not be done with any clownishness or disrespect.

It was about 9:00 p.m. as we stood at the Pali lookout, the technicians setting up lights which ran on portable batteries. The cameraman decided he wouldn't use a fixed tripod position for the video camera—he would hold it using a "live action" style favored by their young audiences. I stood with my back to the railing with the vista of Kaneohe and Kailua beyond. The moon was brightly shining as the clouds seemed fixed in the night sky. Not one gust blew the entire time we were setting up for the shot. The famous breezes of the Pali were resting.

My script was simple. I was to ask in the first segment: "What food must never be taken over the Pali?" Then I was going to answer in the second segment: "Pork!"

We filmed the first segment with no problem. The air remained unusually still. As the reality of the project unfolded, I asked myself how I had gotten involved in such a strange production, but in a few moments I would be finished.

The second segment was also done without a hitch. I said my line flawlessly. However, the producer wanted to do a second take. As we started to re-shoot the segment, the producer suddenly had his assistant bring out a supermarket plastic bag containing a fresh slab of raw pork!

"Hold this, Mr. Grant, please, as you say, 'Pork!'"

"What?" I asked with some concern. "You want me to hold the pork?"

"Yes, that will be very interesting for the audience."

I have been on this earth long enough to know that supernatural entities don't particularly jump out of the bushes at you on a regular basis. I know the difference between urban legend, natural reality and supernatural experience. The "pork over the Pali" is a classic urban legend and I am not overly afraid that something dire will happen to me if I drive my automobile over the Ko'olau with this special meat in my possession. Yet, I have learned to be respectful of supernatural traditions no matter how ludicrous they may sound to others.

"I'm sorry," I told the producer. "You may think this story is funnny or superstitious, but I told you I would not disrespect these traditions. I can't hold the pork and say that."

Very disappointed with me, he tried to argue that it was harmless. He took my place at the railing and tried to show me how it was done. I stepped away as the cameraman came in tight for a close-up of the pork.

From the base of the Pali lookout, a deep, hollow sound suddenly penetrated the night air, roaring up the ancient cliffs to the place where we stood. The blast of wind seemed to come from no where and caught the producer completely by surprise. The pork which had been dangling from his fingertips was caught in the small funnel of wild wind and flew directly into the lens of the video camera. The cameraman was so stunned by the flying meat, that he dropped his very expensive piece of equipment, slightly damaging it. The powerful gust having completed its task, vanished. The air resumed its unnatural calmness.

The production was over as a small film crew from Japan packed up their things and fled the Pali lookout with a new respect for all things uncanny.

THE SACRED ROCKS OF NANAKULI

I n the rock there is life; in the rock there is death." This old
Hawaiian proverb teaches us that the western, scientific
notion that divides the world between things animate and
inanimate is but a point-of-view, not a fixed reality. In the
Polynesian worldview, all things of existence are imbued with
spirit, even a *pohaku* or rock. The spiritual power which a rock
may possess is determined by many factors—the size, shape or
prominence of stones vary just as the size and personalities of
human beings differ. Some stones may have more *mana* or divine
power than others. *Kupua* or demi-gods may reside in one stone,
but not another. The spiritual property in one *pohaku* may benefit
a person's health and well being; another stone may be a *pohaku
wa'uwa'u 'ili*, a rock for attraction or to enhance romance found
offshore at Waikapuna in the district of Ka'u.

In 1997 I was invited to a residential street in Nanakuli to
learn about a rock which in modern times was said to possess
marvelous characteristics. As I arrived at the residence, I was
greeted by a Hawaiian woman in her early forties who had grown
up on Hawaiian homelands in Nanakuli. Her family home was
part of a complex of houses in which her various relatives had
lived since the homelands had been established back in the early
1920's. She politely informed me that the elders who best knew

the stories concerning the rocks on their property would be reluctant to share their tales with a stranger. I assured her that I understood their feelings. In fact, I told her, if she preferred not to tell me the story, keeping it a private family matter, I wouldn't mind at all. In the course of thirty years collecting stories in Hawai'i, I know that as a *haole malihini,* there is a wealth of stories which I will never hear. This is one reason why I never ask anyone for a ghost story—I wait until the story comes to me.

"No," she said to me, "it is all right for me to tell you what happened. I was a little girl at the time, but I still remember everything. My Auntie told me that it was all right to tell you. She sometimes listens to you on the radio telling ghost stories."

She walked me back to the sidewalk, near where I had parked my car. I hadn't noticed it when I had driven up to the house, but on a strip of grass next to the curb there were two large stones embedded in cement. The rocks were about four feet in length and about two or three feet high. Their concrete encasement formed a large section of the curbing.

"When I was a child," she began, "these rocks were actually about four feet over, in the middle of the road. In those days, many of these streets were still unpaved. When it rained the road became like mud. In the summer when it was dry and windy, the road would be like a dust cloud. So back in the 1960's, the city decided to pave and widen the street, and these rocks had to be moved. According to my Aunties, these ancient stones were scared. When a girl began to menstruate, she would come to these stones to make offerings and to sit upon them for protection. These were important stones for young girls changing into women."

I looked down at the rocks with their broad, flat top and remembered that the gender of a Hawaiian *pohaku* was determined by its dominant shape. Vertical stones were male; horizontal stones were female. By that yardstick, both of these stones were female gender.

"When the construction company came down to Nanakuli to widen the road, they moved these rocks first to the side. They never asked nobody about the stones, just figuring they were a couple of ordinary rocks. I guess they used a bulldozer and just pushed them aside.

"The next morning when they came back to work, the rocks overnight had moved right back into their original location in the middle of the road! So they figured maybe somebody was playing a trick on them, so they moved the rocks again. In the morning, the *pohaku* had moved back into their original location!

"Three times they moved those rocks, and three times those rocks moved back. They never wanted to move from where they belonged!"

According to the woman, the owner of the construction company then began to inquire from the neighbors if these rocks had any history. The family who had lived there for many years tried to explain to them how these stones were sacred, especially for young women. Since the expansion and paving of the street was for the benefit of the neighborhood, a *kahuna* or priest was contacted for advice.

He suggested that if the construction company honored the rocks by hosting a large *lu'au* or feast for the neighborhood, the sacred stones may be moved without a problem. Years later the woman could still remember that feast which was given for those stones as one of the best block parties ever held in Nanakuli. All the families were there as they packed several huge pigs in the *imu* or ovens, with tons of fresh fish and *poi*. Hawaiian entertainers performed and the Hawaiian priest gave a special prayer to the rocks which were covered in floral offerings. The stones were then moved to their current location just at the curb of the street.

After the road was widened and paved, the construction company encased the sacred stones in cement. On close inspection I could see in the corner where someone had written in the fresh cement the name of the construction company and the date when these events had taken place.

I thanked the woman for sharing with me her simple, but remarkable tale. On the drive back to Honolulu I enjoyed a wonderful sense of awe at the thought that despite all the modernity that has invaded these Islands, the power of ancient beliefs is still alive, making small miracles still possible.

A Restless Ghost at Queen's Hospital

W hy do the dead come back? Why do apparitions appear to the living? Are they mere "recordings" made of previous lives which mysteriously reappear like the shadowy images on a television screen in the moments after the set has been turned off? Or do they have a purpose to be among us—a message to give? Can they communicate their feelings? A middle-aged local man who spent the night at a Honolulu hospital in the 1930's had an encounter which suggests that the spirits of the dead may not always be even aware that they have passed away!

According to a contemporary newspaper account, the man had gone into the hospital for minor surgery. Placed in a private room in the men's wing of the medical facility, he was alone that night as he went to sleep nervously anticipating the next day's operation.

It was about 10:30 p.m. when he was awakened by a shadowy figure standing next to his bed. It was a Chinese girl about 20 years old who had distinctively bobbed hair in the fashion popular at that time. Her frail body was draped in a plain blue hospital gown, indicating that she was a patient. She placed her hand on his shoulder and spoke to him in a gentle, wispy voice.

"You are in my bed, sir," she said adamantly. "Get out of bed! I want my bed!"

"Excuse me," he responded. "I think you have the wrong room. This is the men's wing."

"Get out of my bed," she repeated more forcefully. "Get out of my bed!"

"Miss, I think you have the wrong room," he again insisted to the disoriented woman. "The women's wing is down on the other side of the building."

"Get out of my bed," she now begged. "I want you out of my bed. That is my bed."

Still a bit groggy-eyed, he sat up in the bed and told the woman standing in the darkened shadow of the room that she really had the wrong room. This wasn't her bed.

"Why don't you get the nurse?" he finally suggested. "Maybe she can fix the problem."

He started to ring for the night nurse when the woman turned and walked away from the bed, appearing to go out the door. The man lay back down, closed his eyes and resumed his sleep. The lost patient, he was confident, would find her missing bed.

About 2:30 a.m., the man awoke again to the movement of someone in the closet. His first thought was that it was the nurse getting a blanket from out of the closet. But when the figure stepped out of the darkness, he saw that it was that lost young Chinese girl again. Hadn't she found her room yet?

He was about to speak to her when she walked up to the foot of his bed. In her right hand, he then noted, was a hanger that she had taken from the closet. For what seemed but a moment their eyes locked on one another. He was so puzzled by her strange demeanor, he found himself suddenly without words. Her pupils were black and as he gazed into them, they seemed to be tiny peepholes into another universe.

"GET OUT OF MY BED!" she suddenly screamed, bring the wire hanger down on his feet.

"GET OUT OF MY BED! GET OUT OF MY BED!"

"You *lolo!*" he screamed. "Get the hell away from me!" He sat up in the bed, attempting to move his feet under the covers so that the stinging blows from the hanger could be avoided.

With one hand he scrambled to push the buzzer that signaled the nurse he needed help. The crazy Chinese girl then dropped the hanger, her slim shadowy form flying through the room and then moving into the wall where it vanished!

A moment later the nurse came rushing through the door to find out what all of the shouting was about. She found the dumb-struck man with his mouth agape, staring transfixed at the wall where the young girl had disappeared.

"Sir, are you all right?" the nurse asked, taking his pulse.

"I think a Chinese girl just went through that wall," he said matter-of-factly. He was still in a state of semi-shock.

The nurse pressed him for an explanation. He described the 20 year old, bobbed-hair Chinese girl in the patient's gown who had been standing beside him earlier that evening. He told the nurse how she had insisted that this was her bed, that she belonged in this bed, not him. He explained how she had hit him with the hanger and then vanished into the wall. He said all these things clearly, in detail and with little emotion, since he could hardly believe his own words.

When he finished his tale, the nurse turned and went running out of the hospital! According to the news story, she left the employment of the hospital, explaining that she would find a job at another medical facility less haunted. She had believed every word of the man's story because she knew something that he did not.

She knew that on the morning before he checked into that room, a young Chinese girl with stylishly bobbed-hair had died following complications from giving birth to a still-born child. Because no one likes to come into a hospital to occupy a mattress where someone else has recently died, she was asked to move the mattress from the women's wing to the men's side of the hospital. Doing as she was told, she placed it in the man's room, turning over the mattress and covering it with sheets. About three hours later, the next patient lay down on the death mattress with absolutely no idea of the tragedy that had so recently occurred on this haunted bedding.

Evidently the young woman had been ripped out of life at a moment which was supposed to have been one of great joy and anticipation—the birth of her first child. Instead of a life of motherhood, she found the emptiness of death, her spirit confused and frightened by the suddenness of her departure from the physical world. In a sense, it may be said, she was not seeking to haunt or harm the man. Bewildered by her unanticipated new condition of death, she may not have even known she had died. She was merely trying to get back onto that mattress, to resume the great journey of life from which she had inadvertently taken an abrupt exit through a one-way turnstile.

THE MYSTERIOUS PLAYMATE

The young Japanese-American couple were beside themselves with glee when they put the down-payment on their first home in the town of Kaunakakai on the island of Moloka'i. Although both of them were originally from O'ahu, they found the rural lifestyle of the so-called "Friendly Island" to be more to their liking than the hustle-and-bustle of Honolulu's city life. They both enjoyed the students they taught at the public schools and how could you beat Moloka'i sweet bread? Their lives seemed moving along on a path unstrewn by disappointment as they set up their new home in a warm, receptive community that reflected all the values they cherished. In a short time, the couple were blessed with a son whom they doted over. Everything seemed to be fitting into place until the fateful day when the mysterious playmate came to visit.

Their son was still a toddler when this unseen companion came to play with him in his bedroom. His mother found her son one day in his room alone, playing with his toys and just babbling away. He spoke to someone, looking at them as if they were actually in the room. This invisible person seemed to accompany their son, however, only in the bedroom. When he went into the living room or outside to play, he never talked with his mysterious playmate. But if he were alone in his room, then the parents could hear the constant chatter between their son and this imaginary friend. Although the child's speech was still a mixture of English and baby-talk, now and then the parents could definitely discern that the boy was answering questions posed by this friend. Their son would ask him a question and then he would burst out laughing as if he had received an answer.

When his parents asked him about his imaginary friend, they had expected their son to answer that he was some cartoon character or perhaps another little boy. They were a bit stunned by his reply.

"The man, Mommie," he would say pointing into the corner of his bedroom. "The man!"

At first this obsession with the "man" seemed charming. Their son seemed to have an active imagination. Perhaps he would grow up to be an author or an artist. Didn't all creative people as children show early signs of genius through their use of the imagination? The charm of their son's new playmate, however, soon faded when the boy suddenly found a new obsession—sleeping with the man.

One late evening, the mother checked in on her son to find him sleeping on the cold floor in the corner where the "man" usually sat. He had gotten out of his bed in the night and curled up in the corner. His body was shivering as they put him back into bed. Later that night, they found their child once again on the floor in the corner, sound asleep with his mysterious playmate. When they asked him why he was going to sleep on the floor, his answer was always the same.

"The man, Mommie," he said pointing in the corner, "the man!"

The obsession of getting out of bed and sleeping with the man continued until finally the father put up a small wire fence around the corner where the alleged "mysterious playmate" lived. If their son wanted to be with him in the daytime, the parents didn't object. But at night, the little fence would go up to prevent the child from sleeping on the floor. Again they urged their son to stay in his bed and not to sleep on the floor.

The fence worked. The first night that he was prevented from sleeping on the floor, the child slept peacefully in his bed throughout the night. He never woke up, cried or attempted to get onto the floor. The second and third night, the fence again worked. Life in their quiet Molokaʻi home had returned to normal.

But by the end of the first week, a new problem developed. The boy was now running a high fever which antibiotics just couldn't bring down. The family physician diagnosed his illness as a mild flu, but the high fever persisted for several days. The sickness must have been caused, the parents concluded, by the boy sleeping on the floor all those nights. The "mysterious playmate" had become suddenly in their minds a very evil influence on the boy. Not only couldn't he now be with the "man" at night, but they insisted that he stop talking to the "man" in the daytime. No more invisible friend was to be allowed, they insisted. The boy seemed bewildered by his parent's anger and spent the day sulking in his room, his fever fluctuating but persistent.

One night at about 11:00 p.m., the parents were in the living room watching late-night television when they heard their son open his bedroom door. Looking toward the hallway, they saw their son walking into the living room. He must be having another restless night due to the fever, they thought, as they asked him if he was all right. He didn't answer, but walked into the room almost as if he was in a trance. He walked right up to the locked front door of the house and silently waited as if the door would somehow open. Although his manner was quiet and restful, there was something about his walk which was extremely puzzling.

As he walked through the room, he raised his right hand into the air as if someone very large was next to him, holding their child's fingers. He seemed to be guided through the living room by an unseen force. When they touched their son, he suddenly burst into tears, frightened and confused. He had no memory of walking out of his bedroom. His forehead was burning with the fever.

"Honey," his mother comforted him, "you have to go back to bed, okay?" Placing him into his bed, they wiped his brow with a cool cloth and took his temperature. The thermometer registered 100 degrees. They gave him an antibiotic as he seemed rested and soon fell back to sleep.

The parents were now very worried as they discussed taking their son to the emergency medical facilities in Kaunakakai. Chills suddenly went down both their backs as they heard their son's door again open. There he was again in that strange trance-like walk, his hand raised high above his head as some large presence guided him to the front door, as if trying to take him away! This time he collapsed when his parents went to wake him up. With his forehead now on fire, the parents wrapped him in a blanket and rushed him to the medical center.

By morning their son's fever had completely broken. For the first time in a week, his spirits seemed cheerful as he ate a big bowl of cereal. The doctor wanted to keep him at the center for the day just for observation, but he anticipated they could take the boy home later that afternoon. When they asked the doctor about their son's strange behavior the night before, he explained it away as a case of sleepwalking. The fever was his concern, not the nocturnal walks which were normal for children of his age.

However, the boy's maternal grandmother didn't find the sleepwalking normal at all. She insisted that before they take the boy back into that house, they have it blessed. They asked some of the long-time Moloka'i residents at the school where they worked, and an old *odaisan* or Japanese spiritual healer who lived on the island was strongly recommended.

The moment the *odaisan* walked into their home, she went straight to the boy's bedroom, pointed at the little fence the father had made around the "mysterious playmate" and ordered that it be taken down immediately.

"Dig up under the house at this place," she explained, "and you will find bones. A man is buried under here."

The father and a neighbor crawled under the house as she instructed, and directly below the corner of the boy's bedroom, they started digging. It took a while maneuvering in the small space that the foundations of the house rested on, but they did find some bones at about the depth of four feet. The bones did indeed appear to be human. The *odaisan* prayed over the bones, making some strange incantations, before the men were ordered to restore them to their grave. The ground was sealed.

She returned to the boy's bedroom where she continued with her prayers, sprinkling salt around the room as she lit several sticks of incense. When she completed her ceremony, she instructed the father to move the child's bed over the place where the bones had been found.

"Never move your son's bed from this corner," she finally explained. "The man who is his friend protects him."

"Protects him from what," the father queried.

"Nightmarchers," she said to their surprise. "There is an ancient path of the spirits of Hawaiian dead that goes through your house on this side of the room. The spirit of the man buried over here had befriended your boy. That is why he was taking him out of the pathway of the nightmarchers. When you forced the boy to say in his bed, then he was in danger. You know, you cannot be on the path of the dead when they walk. You understand that, don't you? You put your boy into danger by keeping him there. The nightmarchers were taking him away."

The "mysterious playmates" which visit children are often explained away by the skeptics as products of an overactive imagination. Everyone at some point in their childhood produces imaginary persons with whom they talk, play and confide their secrets. However, from the spiritual point-of-view, these "mysterious playmates" are sometimes viewed as "guardian angels" or "spirit guides" which provide protection to the child.

So the family took the advice of the *odaisan* and moved their son's bed to the place where his friend was buried. In time, their son stopped playing with his "mysterious playmate" and even forgot who the "man" had been. However, the bones are still buried beneath their home as they believe this "man" protects their boy. And no one ever sleeps on the side of the house where the famous *Ka huaka'i Po* or nightmarchers are said to walk.

THE DRUMS OF KAWAINUI

Mrs. Stacie Healani Acoba is a Honolulu public schoolteacher who lives with her husband in a Kaneʻohe subdivision located near the Kawainui Marsh on the windward side of Oʻahu. They moved into the house in the early 1980's when residential development was expanding the "bedroom" suburbs of Kaneʻohe and Kailua. The house was a modest-sized, modern structure with a back *lanai* that had a lovely view of the vast inland marsh which had become a sanctuary for birds and a few cattle.

In ancient times, Kawainui or "many waters" was a large freshwater pond which was famed for its *oʻopu*, a large, flat mud fish. According to one legend, the people of the district would join hands and dance in the waters to stir up the mud. The fish would then swim to certain people where they would cluster around their legs, making themselves easy to catch. The mud of the pond was also said to be the only edible mud found in Hawaiʻi. With the consistency of *haupia* pudding, this mud was gathered by divers from the bottom of the pond. When this *lepo ai ʻia* or edible mud was collected, no one could say one word, or the diver would be consumed in the mud and drowned. During a shortage of *taro*, it was said that Kamehameha ate the mud from the Kawainui pond. Several ancient *heiau* or temples were located near the pond, including Ulupo Heiau which has been restored on the southside of the marsh, and the unrestored Holomakani Heiau and Moʻokini Heiau, situated on the *mauka* or mountain side.

All this history in their backyard was unfamiliar to Mrs. Acoba until the night she and her husband heard the *pahu* or drums in the far distance being beaten in a distinctive, rhythmic style. It was already after 10:00 p.m. and the noise ordinances were in force as she looked up and down the block. One neighbor's home at the far end of her street had its lights blazing. Assuming this was the offending noise-maker, she called the house to politely ask the family to turn down the music.

"What music?" the neighbor answered.

"You are playing Hawaiian music?" she politely explained, "My husband and I can hear the drums beating from your direction. It's after 10:00 p.m. you know. You can't play it that loud."

"What are you talking about?" the neighbor now insisted. "We aren't playing any Hawaiian music."

"Can you hear those drums then?"

"No," they answered. "We don't hear anything outside."

Mrs. Acoba apologized for disturbing them as she and her husband both heard the drums beating for at least ten minutes more. Then the sound drifted away as the two of them retired to their bedroom. On a still night, they reasoned, maybe the sounds from Kailua wafted over the marsh. Maybe the drums were part of some *hula* concert in town or at one of the schools. Outside only a few crickets could be heard as a gentle wind blew across the marsh and the Acoba's feel into a deep sleep.

The earthquake hit just after 1:00 a.m. The thunderous rumbling of the earth seemed to lift up the house and shake the walls as a stack of books fell off the nightstand. Both of them sat up immediately in their vibrating bed, their minds racing. Where could they get protection if the house collapsed? Again the earth rumbled as a noise against the walls of the bedroom struck the home like the beating of a huge drum. In a moment they realized that the thunderous sound they heard moving through their home like a shockwave was no earthquake. *Pahu* were being beaten all around the walls of their house!

The husband now leaped out of bed, put on a robe and told his wife he would find out who was making all this racket outside. He picked up a thick stick in the kitchen to protect himself and flew out the back door, expecting to encounter the gang of malicious pranksters.

Inside the bedroom, Mrs. Acoba listened to the drumming which never ceased. There was a rhythm to the percussion which sounded similar to the drums they had heard earlier that evening coming from the marsh. A moment later her husband came back into the bedroom, jumped back under the covers and drew them up over both their heads.

"Pray to Jesus, honey," he said, terrified. "There is nobody outside."

For ten more minutes the drumming continued as she and her husband cringed under the blanket. Over and over they repeated the Lord's Prayer until the drumming faded and then finally stopped. Both of them slept with one eye open for the rest of the night.

The next day at work both of them were reluctant to tell anyone what they had heard the previous evening for fear of being considered crazy. But the following night, Mrs. Acoba placed Hawaiian salt at each four corners of the house, and *ti* leaves in the corners of each room. A full dose of Hawaiian spiritual protection, she concluded, was in order for the well-being of her sanity. Every Bible in the house was brought into the bedroom as she and her husband nervously went to sleep the next evening.

The sound of beating drums did not reappear that night. Nor did the terrifying noise reappear the following evening, or the evening after that. In fact during the next two weeks, the strange presence of rhythmically pounding drums emanating from Kawainui Marsh had seemingly vanished, never to return to the Acoba family.

Then on an evening during the third week, a telephone call came late at night from the neighbor who lived up the street in the house which Mrs. Acoba had first surmised the drums were being beaten. Her voice was angry and disturbed.

"This isn't very funny, Stacie," her neighbor complained. "My family can't get any sleep. If this is revenge or something, it is very much beneath you."

"What are you talking about," Mrs. Acoba asked.

"The drums. They are driving us crazy," she explained. "Can you please turn your radio or phonograph down? The drums are coming out of your house and we can't sleep."

It took a little convincing to persuade her neighbor that this was no revenge for the earlier call. Although there was no drumming coming out of her house, the neighbor claimed she heard it coming from the marsh in the direction where the Acobas lived.

The next day Mrs. Acoba telephoned her alma mater, Kamehameha Schools to talk to one of her former Hawaiian history teachers. She informed him of the situation and within a few hours, he escorted an elderly Hawaiian *kahuna* or priest to the subdivision in Kaneʻohe. After examining the area and blessing the property, he explained to Mrs. Acoba that these homes on this street were all located on an ancient pathway of the nightmarchers. The homes were blocking their procession. The drumming which the Acobas had heard were a warning that this place belonged to the spirits of the dead, not the living.

"They are warning each person who lives on this street," the *kahuna* said. "One at a time. It is a warning you must heed."

Upon the advice of the *kahuna*, secret, protective measures were taken at the Acoba home to ensure their safety on the Pokane nights when the dead walk. One by one, each home on this street now must protect itself from the spirit drums which beat their warnings from the ancient waters of Kawainui.

A Choking Ghost in Waikiki

I struggle desperately to get free, but I am tied down by that appalling feeling of helplessness which paralyzes us in our dreams. I want to cry out—but I can't. I want to move—and I can't. Gasping for breath, making terrible, strenuous efforts. I try to turn on my side, try to throw off this creature who is crushing and choking—but I can't!

Then, suddenly, I wake up, panic-stricken, drenched in sweat. I light a candle. I am all alone.

Guy de Maupassant, Le Horla

One of the most prevalent kinds of supernatural experiences in Hawai'i involves what local people often refer to as the "choking" or "pressing" ghost. This frightening sensation usually occurs at the moment when we cross the boundary between full consciousness and the realm of dreams. As described in the 1887 supernatural horror story *Le Horla* by French author Guy de Maupassant, the victim is in a horrifying state of wakefulness, but is unable to move, scream, breathe or call out for help. The sense that some alien creature is sitting upon the victim is sometimes confirmed by the presence of voices or the movement of shadows in the room. In ancient medieval times this experience was attributed to demons called incubus or succubus. These evil entities were often depicted in art as sitting literally on the victim's chest, sucking out the air from their lungs. Some spiritual advisors have cautioned victims of the choking ghost that they were being subjected to a form of a psychic vampirism.

Many cultures have given names to this choking ghost. Hawaiians referred to an *akua noho,* a god who possesses the living by sitting or pressing down upon them. In Japan the "tie-down ghost," called *kanashibari,* is still extremely prevalent among both genders and all classes of individual. The sensation is well-known in Canada and Newfoundland where it is termed "hagging." The origin of the term is linked to beliefs that witches or Old Hags were responsible for these nightmarish attacks which even Shakespeare referred to in Romeo and Juliet:

This is the hag, when maids lie on their backs,
That presses them, and learns them first to bear,
Making them women of good carriage:

In recent times, these symptoms have been medically explained as forms of "sleep paralysis" or nacrolepsy. Psychologist J.A. Cheyne of the University of Waterloo in a study which links sleep paralysis to the current stories of "alien abduction," has noted that the paralysis may last from a few seconds to several minutes or possibly longer. "This is not a dream state," he writes, "although it is frequently confused with such, because those subject to this experience are not asleep but awake, and usually very alert." Most importantly, the victim is fully aware of their surroundings during the experience, confirming that the encounter is not a dream or hallucination.

In the course of collecting first-hand accounts of a pressing ghost in Hawai'i, the pattern seems often the same: being awakened in the middle of the night by some force pressing upon the victim's chest. However, in one story told to me by a visitor to Waikiki in the early 1980's, the choking ghost can take many varied forms.

A frequent visitor to the Islands from California due to interstate business dealings, he often stayed at a prominent Waikiki hotel without incident. Like many of the victims of the "choking ghost," he also insisted that he never had had any paranormal experiences during his life. He had very little interest in ghosts, afterlife or the supernatural. Due to the fact that he came to Hawai'i on business, he usually stayed alone in a room with a single bed.

The evening of his unusual encounter he had gone to bed at about 10:00 p.m. to get rested for an important meeting in the morning. It was about two hours later that he woke up in great discomfort. The mattress that he was lying on had become so lumpy that he couldn't find a place to comfortably rest his body. He tossed and turned, moving about the mattress trying to get rested when suddenly he realized that his problem wasn't simply faulty mattress springs. Underneath him, literally positioned within the mattress, he felt another human body pressing up. The "lumps" were actually the chest, legs, arms and head of a powerful human form moving up through the bed itself!

As he began to leap off the mattress, the entity from inside the mattress grabbed his naked thighs with a powerful, ice cold sensation. The victim tried to call out for help when a powerful, frozen hand cupped his mouth, preventing him from breathing. It was as if this creature in the bed had a dozen hands that reached up and around him, pulling him back to the bed. Then the cold hands gripped his throat and began choking him from behind. Unable to now move, breathe or scream, he felt helpless but to succumb to a horrible cloud of death drifting over him. Then, as quickly as the threatening hands had appeared, they vanished. The lumps within the bed also disappeared as the visitor was left sweating and frightened on the unholy mattress. In that one moment of horror, he had joined a fraternity of ten thousand others who will forever live with a haunted memory of a "choking" ghost.

The Mejiro Bird

The Nakashima family lived in the small village of Kapoho in the district of Puna on the Big Island in the days before electricity reached that remote farm country. A small, tight-knit family, the Nakashimas eked out a living from selling the papaya they cultivated on their several-acre farm in this verdant section of the island. Without a radio, television or a daily newspaper in the village, their lives largely consisted of work, Sunday services at the Pahoa Honpa Hongwangji Buddhist Temple and fishing the waters along the Puna coast. In the seclusion of their island lives, it hardly seemed possible that a "police action" taking place half-way around the globe in Korea could reach into this peaceful village and snatch up one of their beloved sons.

Yet Sam "Abe Lincoln" Nakashima never complained when he received his draft notice from the United States Army. Although he wasn't entirely certain why the United Nations had become involved in the conflict between North and South Korea, he was a patriot who believed that it was his national duty to risk his life for the freedom he and his family enjoyed in little Kapoho village. In fact, as a teenager going to school Sam had loved American history class so much, he mounted portraits of Abraham Lincoln and George Washington on the wall above his bed. At one point, he even grew a beard, shaving it in a fashion to resemble Lincoln. From then on, his friends nicknamed him "Abe Lincoln" Nakashima.

It was several months after "Abe Lincoln" had gone to fight for his country when a peculiar thing happened one evening in the Nakashima home. The family had just sat down together for dinner, when a tiny mejiro bird flew right into the home through the open, screenless window, sailed past the living room and into Sam's bedroom. The bird fluttered over his bed, turned and flew back through the living room and landed on the back of an empty chair placed at the dining table. For nearly a minute the bird sat on its perch, peacefully looking at all the members of the startled Nakashima family. Then the tiny bird flew out the window and soared away.

The next morning, Sam's brother found the little mejiro bird in the kerosene hurricane lamp which was kept on the mantle in the living room. The bird was dead. No one had seen it fly into the house; no one had seen it in the living room. How the bird got into the lamp was a mystery.

Later that day, the mystery intensified when the brother went into the bedroom he shared with Sam to find the portrait of Abraham Lincoln turned upside down on the wall. When he tried to straighten the portrait, he discovered that it couldn't be moved. The wire used to hang the picture had been twisted around the nail in the wall so tightly, that it couldn't be moved. Someone had turned the portrait over and over until the wire hanger was tightened on the nail! No one in the Nakashima family had been in the room the entire day. There was no logical way that the portrait of Abraham Lincoln could have been turned in such a bizarre fashion.

Two days later, a drab, khaki-colored automobile with a single white star on the door drove up to the front of the Nakashima homestead. A somber man in a military uniform got out of the vehicle and walked up to the door to tell Papa Nakashima that his eldest son Private Samuel Nakashima was missing in action in Korea. Trapped with his unit in heavy fighting following an ambush by Northern Korean troops, he and five other men were believed to be either dead or taken prisoner. At this point the U.S. Army was uncertain. The

Nakashimas, however, would be personally notified the moment any further information became available.

The days passed into weeks at Kapoho Village as life continued unchanged except for the missing presence of "Abe Lincoln" Nakashima. Prayers for their missing son were offered every morning and night at the family *obutsudan* or altar. While the family waited for news of their beloved Sam, Papa Nakashima had gone one weekend with some of his friends to Ka La'e or South Point on the Big Island. Despite the grief he felt for his missing son, the family still needed their fish to survive. At sunrise he was alone on the rocky shore, casting out his net when he saw suddenly a woman in a snow-white *kimono* standing not twenty feet away from him.

What was she doing out in this remote area? he thought to himself. There was no one living anywhere near this southernmost tip of the Big Island. She seemed almost to radiate with light as he saw her lift out her hands in which she delicately held a small mejiro bird. The tiny creature flew up from the palms of the woman's hands toward Papa Nakashima, passed his shoulder and then soared up to the heavens where it vanished. In a moment, the woman was gone. The father knew that his son had come to say once again, for a final time, "*sayonara*."

When the officer returned to the Nakashima home a few weeks after this incident with the news of Sam's death, the family was already prepared for the sad news. His remains were returned to Hawai'i, and buried in the veteran's cemetery in Hilo. The lives of the Nakashima family never entirely returned to normal with the chair left vacant by the death of Sam "Abe Lincoln" Nakashima. But whenever a mejiro bird flew over their Kapoho home, the faith of a future reunion fluttered with those tiny wings.

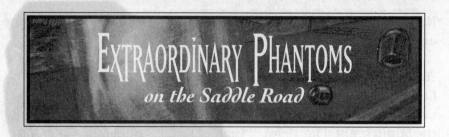

Extraordinary Phantoms
on the Saddle Road

E very once in a while, the tales of extraordinary supernatural occurrences are reported in the local newspapers as investigated fact. While the explanations behind the phenomenon are beyond the boundaries of objective news reporting, the fact that eye witnesses to these odd events are willing to come publicly forward attests to the veracity of their statements. This was especially true in 1969 when the Honolulu newspapers covered a series of remarkable tales circulating on the Big Island of Hawai'i concerning poltergeist activities on the famed Saddle Road.

The time was just before midnight and the place was a desolate stretch of the Saddle Road that connects Hilo to the west side of Hawai'i across the island interior's lunar landscape. Taxi driver Pedro Monzano was returning to Hilo Airport after dropping a Parker Ranch employee at Humu'ula. Lava stones strewn across the road caused one of his tires to blow out.

After removing the lug nuts from his damaged tire, Pedro threw the wrench into the trunk of his car. As he lifted the spare tire onto the wheel, an bizarre thing happened.

"I tightened the lug nuts when I hear a noise on the right side," he later told reporters. "I see the wrench. I stand up one time and look around. Nobody there."

Somehow, the wrench which had been in the car had moved out of the trunk to Pedro Monzano's side. Although terrified, he said out loud to no one in particular, "Thank you, very much." He then finished tightening his spare, jumped into his taxi, and sped to Hilo to spread the word about the ghostly doings on the Saddle Road.

Pedro Monzano wasn't alone in "seeing things" during February of 1969. A group of Department of Education teachers traveling on the Saddle Road earlier had seen eerie lights along the road. As they pulled over to examine the unusual phenomena, the strange fires vanished.

Akualele, or flying gods, explained the Hawaiians of the Big Island. These fireballs that fly in the night are sometimes omens of approaching death. Local Japanese identified them as *hinotama* or the fires of disembodied spirits.

The unearthly happenings on the Saddle Road did not begin with flying wrenches and fireballs. The Henry Macomber family, returning to Waiki'i from Hilo on the evening of January 31, 1969, saw two yellowish-red lights in the distance resembling an approaching car. The lights came closer, then suddenly vanished. Turning the pick-up truck around to return to Hilo, the family was suddenly struck by an invisible force that rocked the vehicle violently. The terrified family then fled the scene of their supernatural encounter.

Henry Macolmber later described for reporters how this powerful push seemed to have a mass. It struck the tarpaulin on the window, banged on the sides of the truck and rapped on the hood, he insisted.

Earthquakes? Swamp gas? Overactive imaginations? Despite the theorizing of Big Island scientists, no plausible explanation was given to Pedro Monzano, the teachers or the Macombers. What force could violently shake a pick-up truck or lift a wrench out of a trunk and throw it several feet? What are the *akualele* that Hawaiians for centuries have seen in the darkness of the night? What otherworldliness continues to haunt the Saddle Road?

When Barbara Pacheco and her friends were driving that quiet highway across the saddleback of the Big Island in 1970, they of course had heard all of these stories concerning the strange lights on that eerie road. But to save time that evening, they decided to use the Saddle Road to get back to Hilo before midnight. Since the two-lane highway is dangerous in some areas where the pavement is ill-kept, the dips sudden and the curves sharp, she drove at a safe 40 miles per hour. The car behind her, however, was moving at far too fast a speed. Its headlights which had originally appeared as tiny specks in the rearview mirror, were now rapidly approaching.

"Hey," said one of the passengers in the rear, "watch out for that car! The guy is driving like an idiot."

Barbara tried to slow down and pull over so the car behind could pass safely. All of them watched as it pulled around next to them, accelerated and then cut dangerously in front of them. Several of the people inside Barbara's car made a certain hand gesture reserved for poor drivers. The reckless driver continued speeding up ahead of them, came to a turn in the road and flipped over. The automobile burst into a ball of fire and smoke as a horrified Barbara drove her car through the scene of the terrible accident. It was at least 200 feet further into the curve that she could herself pull over and turn around so that they could render assistance to anyone left alive in the explosion of gasoline and flame. Everyone inside her vehicle was stunned, their hearts racing as they braced themselves for the human carnage which awaited.

As they came back into the turn from the opposite direction, expecting to find the fiery vehicle, they were amazed to discover that the fire was no longer burning. The thick black smoke had totally cleared. And the automobile which they had witnessed crashing into the desolate field of lava had totally vanished. There was not a trace of another living soul on that stretch of highway through the moon-like terrain of the mysterious Big Island.

THE LOST FISHERMAN
As Told by Helen Fujie

On a beautiful Sunday morning in 1972 my brother-in-law, Eiji Funada, husband of my husband's sister Tsuchiyo, went on a fishing trip outside of Kaumalapau Harbor on the southwest coast of Lana'i.

He was accompanied by a Mr. Sagawa who wanted to pick *opihi* at the landslide area. So Eiji left his friend ashore and went out by himself to fish in the deep waters further south.

Eiji anchored way out there and fished a while but decided to start the engine to go back to pick up Mr. Sagawa.

According to Mr. Sagawa, something was tricky about the throttle of the engine. Evidently, when Eiji tried to crank up the engine, the boat suddenly shot forward. Eiji was thrown backwards over the side of the boat and became tangled in the trailing fish lines behind.

When a Maui fishing boat came by, the men aboard saw a small boat circling around at a fast speed with a man dangling at the end of the fishing lines. They couldn't get near the boat to rescue the man, so they went into Kaumalapau Harbor to notify the game wardens, police, and firemen. A rescue crew was sent to the scene of the accident.

By the time the crew reached the boat, it had run out of gas and stood floating deathly still. However, there was no man at the end of the rope. Since these were shark-infested waters, the body of Eiji may have been devoured by those silent carnivores of the ocean.

The men searched the area until sundown and couldn't find Eiji. Finally, the search was called off. A call was made to Eiji's life insurance agent and the doctor to proclaim him dead...his body lost at sea.

That night all the neighborhood friends with jeeps and boats volunteered to search the shoreline for the missing man's body. The next morning at dawn all of the volunteers were to meet at the Funada's home for breakfast.

His wife Tsuchiyo and his sister, Mrs. Ito, put up a Buddhist shrine in the parlor and slept in front of it that night. My husband did not want to sleep on the floor with the two women, so he went home to his own bed. I stayed back to sleep with my sister-in-law.

In the middle of the night, in the wee hours of the morning, two huge hands suddenly pressed me down to my mattress.

"No need," a voice spoke in the darkness. It was Eiji's voice. He kept saying, "No need! No need!" over and over. I struggled to get up as the hands pressed me down.

"I have to wake up now," I said out loud, arguing with his spirit. "I have to make coffee for the men who are going to search for you!"

Eiji kept pushing me and choking me, just his huge hands and his voice saying, "No need!" I did not see his face nor his body.

His sister sleeping next to me shook me awake to say, "Helen, you're having a nightmare! You're arguing and struggling to get up!" I told her quietly that her brother had pushed me down saying, "No need!"

His body was never found. Just as he had tried to tell me, he would always be lost at sea. So with no death certificate or remains, a memorial service was conducted for Eiji Funada with only his picture.

A RADIO SPIRIT

As Told by Charlie Doremus

C harlie Doremus has no concrete physical proof that the ghostly encounter ever actually happened. He made no recordings of the supernatural electronic message which was perhaps aired that evening many years ago. Yet he remains convinced that the spirit of the dead did communicate to the living through a simple radio with the dial set on the world of Chicken Skin.

Electronic Voice Phenomenon or EVP is a well-known category of supernatural occurrences which have attracted both serious-minded parapsychologists as well as quacks throughout the last century. If the disincarnate spirits of the dead are linked to this world through psychic powers, then could that energy be channeled through electronic devices such as the telephone, radio or television? Thomas Alva Edison announced that he was working on an electronic telephone which would make direct contact with the dead—a device which was evidently never completed before his death. In the 1959, a Swedish opera singer and film producer Friedrich Jurgenson claimed that during the tape recording of bird calls made in the countryside of his villa in Sweden, he inadvertently recorded the voice of a spirit who gave him messages from the other world. In the 1960s, the psychologist and philosopher Konstantin Raudive continued

Jurgenson's experiments, claiming that he had recorded over 10,000 spirit voices.

The Society for Psychical Research in London examined the Raudive tapes and concluded that the EVP evidence was highly subjective. The sounds made by alleged spirits could be interpreted as natural phenomenon. That the claims of EVP experimenters were similar to the Rorschach tests of visual phenomenon—one sees in a picture what one wants to see.

The electronic message which Charlie Doremus believes was sent from the spirit world was sent in January of 1975, following the death of his grandmother at the age of 74 years in her home in New Jersey. His grandmother had been suffering from a lingering illness for several months. Charlie at that time was living in Pittsburgh, Pennsylvania. Having been very close to his grandmother, he left work and traveled to New Jersey to be there with her at the end.

After she died, Charlie telephoned his girl friend in Pittsburgh and asked her if she would come up to New Jersey to be with him at the funeral. She agreed and was able to provide him much comfort during his grief. Then on the night before they were scheduled to return home to Pittsburgh, his girlfriend asked him a very unusual question.

"What does 'Rosen Jim' mean to you, Charlie?"

"'Rosen Jim'?" he replied. "That was the name of the boat my grandparents used to go fishing on when I was a youngster. How do you know that name?"

"I just heard a woman talking on the radio," his girlfriend answered. "She used the name 'Rosen Jim' and talked about your old neighborhood. You know, the place where you told me you grew up. She was talking about all of those things."

At first Charlie thought the whole thing sounded a little crazy. Why would people be talking about a fishing boat that had sunk many years before? The strange thing was that he had never spoken to his girlfriend about the Rosen Jim or anything related to that boat.

On a hunch, he then pulled out an old recording of his grandmother and played it for his girlfriend. As she listened to his deceased grandmother's voice, her face turned sheet-white.

"That's the woman from the radio!" she gasped.

Charlie's girlfriend and grandmother had never met or spoken. Yet that night as they listened to that old recording, she insisted that the voice she had heard on the radio and the voice on the tape were one and the same. There was only one copy of the tape with his grandmother's voice. Charlie was the only person, other than his deceased grandmother who even knew the tape had been made. And how had his girlfriend known the name of that old fishing boat? The only answer to his questions seemed both crazy and impossible. But he was still persuaded that his grandmother that night had tried to reach out from the grave using that radio to let him know she had survived her death.

THE DROWNING POOL OF HAWAI'I

I s Waimea Falls haunted?" the Honolulu daily newspaper reporter asked curiously. "Do you have stories about unusual things happening there?"

"Yes," I answered straightforwardly. "There are many stories about the pond. Why?"

"There has been another drowning there," she continued, "and when I was doing the background research on earlier deaths associated with the pond. . . I felt something was a little strange. What is the story you know about the pond?"

In the *Obake Files*, I explained to her, I had shared a story which is my "most authentic" ghost story since it is the only tale I have ever collected which was given to me with a copy of the police report verifying the facts as reported by retired Honolulu Police Department officer "Buddy" Aldophson. It is not often that a ghost story comes with an official document proving its veracity.

I told her the full story which Officer Aldophson had first shared with me in 1986 as we sat not one hundred feet from that ancient pool of sacred waters. It was a tale which began on July 26, 1952, when Bill Lawrence, a merchant marine from Seattle jumped from the 40 foot top of Waimea Falls into the pond below. As his four mainland friends watched horrified, Bill missed his footing, hit his head on the side of the cliff and slammed into the pond with a loud snapping sound. A later autopsy would reveal that he broke his neck and probably died instantly.

His friends instantly dove into the dark waters to get their friend. They dove again and again, but they could not find his remains. About ten minutes later, they told the police, his back suddenly popped up out of the water. They could see only the tip of his shoulder blades—his head, arms, legs, and torso were twisted in the water in such a way that only the back was sticking up. He was probably jack-knifed in the water.

They quickly swam over to retrieve him, praying he was still alive. Then just as they got within a couple of feet of his floating remains, his body violently began to shake in the water, twisted then sank like a brick to the bottom of the pond. It was so sudden, it seemed literally as if someone had grabbed his trunks and yanked him back into the water.

Again his friends dove in after him to no avail. Their friend had vanished. At three o'clock the Honolulu Police Department at the Hale'iwa Police Station got a call that their friend had drowned at Waimea Falls. Sergeant Aldolphson went out there with a dozen volunteers and some firemen in a rescue team to recover the corpse. They had ten-foot poles with hooks at the end which they used to dredge the bottom of the murky waters. Divers tried to locate the body with no luck. Nets were dropped and pulled through the water to no avail. That day no body was found at the bottom of the pond.

The pond was only about 12 to 15 feet deep that summer. The diameter is only about 25 to 30 feet. Despite that fact that the pond was not that deep or large, the body of Bill Lawrence could not be found. It had seemingly disappeared. The sergeant told me that in his career with the HPD, he would pull many bodies out of that pond. However, most of them had vanished for two or three days before they were recovered. It was one of the strange things about that pond which he never quite could figure out. Try as you might to find them, bodies just vanished in the pond! Then a couple of days later, there the corpse was just floating on the surface. Where's it been for all that time?

Sometimes when the water had emptied from the pond, the Sergeant would walk around the bottom searching for an underwater rock ledge, a cave or an underwater stream that connects to the pond—anything that could help to explain why bodies would not float but get stuck at the bottom. No such evidence of any ledge, cave or stream could be found. There was one pointed, pyramidal rock, he explained, that had once been on the bottom of the pond. On one occasion, a diver had slammed his head into the pointed tip of the stone. With the rock point embedded in his head, the victim was held underwater until he was found hours later. That stone, however, had been removed as a precaution. Nothing else could explain the strange disappearances in the drowning pool.

By sunset of July 26, 1952, the body of Bill Lawrence has still not been recovered. The valley was already getting dark when Sergeant Aldolphson and his men called it quits for the day. Concerned about the well-being of the four other merchant marines, the Sergeant offered them a place to stay at his house in Hale'iwa.

"No, Sergeant," they answered. "We'll stay here at the pond overnight. If Bill's body comes up, we'll pull him out. We don't want any animals to eat him."

So the Sergeant left the four *haole* men setting up camp at the pond as he and his crew hiked out of the valley. In the morning when they returned, they were surprised to see the merchant marines nearly running out of Waimea Valley.

"Glen," he said to me, "I saw the four most scared *haole* I've ever seen in my life come running down that valley. They were white the day before, but you should have seen them that morning! They were like shark bait!"

"What in the hell happened to you guys?" the Sergeant asked.

"Last night something attacked us, Sergeant," they said nervously.

"Attacked you? What in the world are you talking about?"

After the Sergeant left the valley, they explained, they had camped right near the pond. About 10:00 p.m. something came out of the pond. It moved out of the water and then began to move in the bushes. The men could hear this thing stalk them. As it moved about in the bushes, this thing would suddenly grab a brush, shake it violently and then jump over them with a splash into the pond.

Fifteen minutes later, the thing came out again, stalking them, shaking bushes and then leaping back into the pond. Then, at about 1:00 a.m. in the morning it began to make a horrible, tortured noise. Since the Sergeant was a hunter who had lived and hunted in the North Shore area most of his life, he knew every animal that lived in the wild. And some of them did make strange noises.

"Listen, you guys," he said reassuringly. "You tell me the noise and I'll tell you the animal, because there are dogs and pigs and cats and birds and all other kind of wild life in the valley."

The sound from the pond that these men then replicated convinced the Sergeant that this had been no pig. For the men claimed that a series of horrible, guttural screams came out of the water that night which were the torment of a soul tortured in some pit of hell. Imagine the pain one would feel having their flesh flayed from their body alive. Then multiply that horror by ten. This was the sound which came from the pond in Waimea Valley on July 27, 1952 at 1:00 a.m.

The Sergeant and the crew looked at one another with raised eyebrows. Either those *haole* guys were the best storytellers they had ever met, or some human being in the valley had been tortured in the valley the night before.

"Come on," the Sergeant said to the men, "we got a job to do. Let's get that boy's body and then get out of there."

As they approached the pond, the Sergeant told me that his mouth dropped. In his whole life he has never seen Waimea Falls pond as crystal clear and mirror-smooth as he had seen it that morning. Usually the water was dark and murky from the sediment washing off from the walls of the cliff. But that morning the water was as clear and still as a glass of clean water. It was so clear, they could all see the bottom of the pond.

Feeling very lucky that they would find the body of Bill Lawrence in the clear water, the Sergeant and the volunteers looked everywhere on the bottom of the pond. The remains of the victim were nowhere to be found. So the Sergeant climbed up to the top of the waterfall, hoping to see the body from a higher vantage point. It was about 30 minutes later that he did at last see the body laying face-down on a big, flat stone not far from the edge of the pond where his men were standing. The arms were placidly positioned at the side of the corpse.

"I see the body!" he called to his men on the walkie-talkie. "He's on a big rock about ten feet from where you're standing."

"We see the rock," the men called back up, "but we don't see any body."

"Lower your hooks and just try to catch him," the Sergeant instructed. The hooks were then dropped, and dredged across the top of the large stone that resembled an altar.

"Okay! We got 'em!" the men finally called out. "We got 'em."

The body which had not been visible from the side of the pond was now clearly seen as the grappling hooks pulled him off his bier. The Sergeant used a portable two-way radio to call the coroner in Hale'iwa.

"We found the victim," he told the medical officer. "Bring out the wagon and we'll meet you at Waimea Beach."

Just then, the Sergeant hung up the radio, looked back down at his crew lifting the body out of the water and he felt an electrical shock go through his body. The hair on his head and arms shot up as if he had plugged himself into an electrical outlet. The adrenaline pumped through his heart as he watched something come up from the pond, following the feet of Bill Lawrence.

"What in the hell? What is it, Sergeant?" his men screamed, backing away from the water. "What's going on?"

Looking up the valley, he could see that the water in the stream had not increased its volume. The water in the falls had not risen but slowly trickled over at the same rate. But there where the feet had been pulled out of the pond was a two-foot column of water rising like a fountain. The water was churning wildly and lifting from the pond as if trying to follow the feet of the corpse.

The Sergeant then watched from his safe perch as the fountain expanded in size. Three feet, four feet, five feet, until it seemed the entire pond was a raging, boiling pot of water. Then there appeared at the bottom of the pond a motion like two great arms moving back and forth. The pond was transforming into a giant washing machine with the agitator speeding up faster and faster as if it was out of control. The water was lifting along the sides of the steep cliff.

"GET THE HELL AWAY FROM THE POND!" he screamed as his men picked the victim's body up and started running down the valley. They got about 200 feet from the pond, when they looked back to see an eight foot tsunami chasing them down the valley! The pond had literally erupted, the water violently emptying out within minutes. The tidal wave hit them like a locomotive, picked them up and spewed them out of the mouth of the valley. Everything in the water's path was cleared out as the worst flood in a decade destroyed the lower part of the valley. The pond had completely emptied itself as new, fresh water from upstream slowly refilled the void.

Fortunately nobody was killed in the flood and the body was recovered. But what freak accident of nature could have caused such flooding? The Sergeant went to the University of Hawai'i where he showed his police report to a seismologist— had there been any earth tremors which could explain the strange flood? According to the scientist, the island of O'ahu was still at the moment the pond erupted. There had been no rains or flash flooding in the *mauka* area behind the falls. In fact, the scientist told the Sergeant, there was no rational explanation for the description of events as contained in the police report. The look in the man's eyes suggested that the Sergeant had fabricated the entire episode.

The only reasonable explanation he was ever given for the events of July 26-17, 1952 came from an old Hawaiian *kupuna* who had lived all of his life in the North Shore. When he heard the Sergeant's story, he calmly explained what had happened to Bill Lawrence and the drowning pool.

"Sergeant," he said wisely, "I think you wen' took out the body too soon. The *akua* had to throw out the *lepo* from the *haole* boy."

As the Sergeant understood the old man, the pond at Waimea Valley had an *akua* or god who occasionally desired human sacrifice. When people jump into the pond, they do not understand that the waters are used in sacred ritual. The body was taken down to the *ahu* or altar, the large flat rock on the bottom of the pond, where the ceremony is performed. Human sacrifice rituals lasted for several days in ancient times, the length of time that the bodies are frequently missing in the water.

After the *akua* is finished with the ritual, the human remains would then be disposed of—at the time the bodies reappeared.

When the Sergeant pulled the body off the rock within 24 hours, the *kupuna* concluded, the ritual was not finished. The *lepo* or waste from the ceremony was still on the altar. So the *akua* stirred the water up, washed off his altar and then threw the bad water out so that fresh, clean water could fill the pond.

When I finished retelling the story in condensed fashion to the reporter from the daily newspaper, she indicated that she had heard from others about the "altar rock" on the bottom of the pond. Yet, it wasn't just the recent accident or legend of the sacrificial stone that had prompted her to call me. She was puzzled by something else which at that time came as a great surprise to me.

"Did you know," she asked me, "that the demographic profile of the victims in the last fifty years are startlingly similar?"

"What do you mean?"

"People who drown in the pond are the same age, gender, race and occupation! And they all drown at the same time of the year!"

"What?" I said as the hair on my arm rose. As much as I had thought about doing this type of project, I had never had the time to research the history of drownings in the pond. The reporter had done a preliminary background check and was obviously disturbed by what she had found.

Caucasian males, between the ages of 18-25 years old who are in the military are the most likely candidates for drowning in the pond during the late summer months. Of course, being *malihini* to Hawai'i and having no knowledge of the pond's dangers, they may be more inclined to act recklessly around the falls. Their military background and youthfulness may add to their need to demonstrate their "machismo" in a daredevil manner. All these factors may contribute to the fact that this small group of males have a disproportionate standing in the percentage of people who have died in the drowning pool.

However, I add a bit of historical background to the reporter's fascinating inquiry into the mystery of this pond. The old name for the falls was not Waimea. The older name was Waihe'e, a

name associated with a warrior and *kahuna* or priest by the name of Koi who had been given this valley in the days of Kahekili during the eighteenth century. Kahekili was the great chief of Maui who extended his powerful rule to Oʻahu, dividing up the control of the island among his favorite chiefs. Koi was from Wailuku where he maintained the Waiheʻe *heiau*, a sacred temple where human sacrifice was performed. The name given to the falls is the same name as that of this temple where this fierce warrior made human offerings to his gods of war and conquest.

At Waimea Valley, Koi assembled a powerful army of men who were like himself *pahupu*, "cut in two" warriors. Samuel M. Kamakau describes them as "strange-looking men tattooed black from top to toe, with eyelids turned inside out and help up by props and only their eyeballs and teeth left in their natural state." In May 12, 1792, the storeship *Daedalus* of Captain George Vancouver's squadron, visited Waimea Bay. Four men went ashore to collect freshwater, including Commander Lt. Hergest, the astronomer William Gooch and two seaman. As they hiked into the valley, they were ambushed by the *pahupu* warriors. The body of William Gooch and two other men were then taken to Puʻu-o-mahuka *heiau* on the upper ridge overlooking the valley where rituals of human sacrifice were performed.

William Gooch, by the way, was a twenty-one old Caucasian military officer in the British Navy.

The reporter gave out a long sigh as we both pondered the mysterious way in which coincidences sometimes take a firm grasp upon the imagination. The conclusion to this tale is yours, dear reader, as you wonder what unknown force awaits, as you take that long leap into the dark and murky drowning pool beneath your feet.

KEOLA'S DREAM

Tom and Alana Correira with their four-year-old son Keola moved into their new Nu'uanu cottage in 1971. An historic house located on a quiet street with little traffic, all three of them loved their new home. It was a far cry from where the young family had been living on Cleghorn Street in the heart of the old Waikiki "jungle." Keola now had friends in this small, friendly neighborhood whom he could play with every afternoon until the sun disappeared. The house was built sometime during the last century, and the interior walls all had a natural finish to them with a large built-in bookcase in the parlor. A twin bed which was used by Keola was located under the bookcase. Although the Correiras brought in most of the furniture, a rattan dining table accompanied by two chairs and a rattan lounge chair came with the house.

This was the sort of picture-perfect house for a young, professional family beginning their life together in a tranquil Honolulu valley. Isn't it amazing how all of this can be shattered by dark, unseen forces which visit this world not from a motive of meanness, but from an eternal suffering unresolved?

Many years after the events had taken place, I interviewed Tom Correira concerning his unforgettable encounter with the supernatural at this rented Nu'uanu Valley cottage. His story was rich in detail, revealing how these ghostly experiences remain indelibly fixed on the human memory. The following are his words concerning the tale he chose to call "Keola's Dream:"

I'll never forget that house. Although it was basically a simple one-bedroom cottage, it had a few unique features about it. First, it was filled with windows—windows, windows, windows. These were the old-fashioned kind of windows that you can lift the bottom part up or the top part down. They were all framed with four glass panes to the top and four to the bottom part of the window. There were 18 windows in all. For a one-bedroom place, that meant a whole lot of eyes.

The second odd aspect of the house was a bathroom located in the bedroom closet. For in addition to the regular bathroom with its built-in shelves for linen and towels, a shower and basin had been installed in a tiny closet in the bedroom. The shower was about the size of a box that fits a fifty-gallon water heater. The basin had to be used sideways because if you tried to bend over and wash your face using it the normal way, your *okole* would hit the door. "Small" is too big to describe that very weird bathroom.

Finally, adjacent to the living room was another room which was too little to be called it a bedroom. This "alcove" had another window and a closet. However, I could never figure out what the purpose of the room was because you couldn't even fit a twin bed into this room. The top part of the window looked out the back of the house where an old banyan tree was planted. The 100-year-old tree was at least forty feet high. For some reason, the bottom part of the main trunk was blackened out with paint. This tree was huge and it partially draped itself over the cottage, creating a large shadow that kept the cottage cool for most of the day. Some days when a strong wind would blow through the valley, the rustling of its leaves made it almost impossible for hearing casual conversation. In this alcove of wasted space, we decided to store all of Keola's toys.

The first year in the Nu'uanu cottage was really wonderful. It was only into the second year that weird things started to happen.

I remember one afternoon watching television, smoking a cigarette and enjoying some time with my wife. All of a sudden,

I couldn't breath! It was as if I had forgotten how to perform the most vital biological function to live! I must have started to panic, because my wife looked at me sensing that something was wrong. She asked if I was all right, but it seemed like ten minutes before I could even answer her, gasping for breath. I was literally blue when finally the air filled my lungs.

When I told my wife that I had felt like I had forgotten how to breath, she couldn't stop laughing. I told her it wasn't funny. I had felt like something or someone was holding me back from breathing. It was like a choking sensation when you can neither inhale or exhale. When she saw how serious I was about the incident, she finally stopped laughing and shared my concern about how weird the episode had truly been.

A couple of months went by without incident until the evening I returned home from work at about 11:30 p.m. My wife was still up working on some papers for the next day at work. She told me to sit in the chair that she was sitting in and look into the bottom left window pane across the room from where she was sitting. I did as she instructed, but saw nothing. She sat in the chair, looked and saw nothing. She then told me that all night long, right up until the time I sat in her chair, she would be working on her papers looking down, when out of the side of her eye she swore she saw a woman looking in at her. When she'd look up, the woman's face would disappear. When she would return to her work the woman's face would show up in a different pane in a different window. Finally she decided to ignore it until I got home.

To be honest, I thought it had only been her imagination. I thought nothing of it and made her a bit mad by chuckling at her fear. Before we went to bed that night, she went over to Keola's bed to kiss him on the cheek. When she came back to the bedroom, she told me that Keola had a wonderful smile on his face as if he was laughing in his sleep.

"If only I could dream like that," I told her as we both went to sleep.

The Christmas holidays were soon upon us. My wife had to go on a business trip to the mainland for her company. One night while she was away and Keola was staying over at his grandmother's house, I was lying on the living room floor watching television. As the night went on I remember dozing in and out of whatever show I was watching. It was well after midnight when I thought I awoke and seemed to hear a low-pitched buzzing or humming kind of noise. I wasn't sure if I was only in dream-like state of mind. When the buzzing started to get louder, I realized I was not dreaming at all, but was actually wide awake. I tried to move my arms but they were not responding. Thinking maybe I was still dreaming, I again tried to move my body. Again nothing happened. The buzzing or humming was getting louder as my eyes were now fully opened. I was fully awake and now in a real panic. I couldn't move. I lay there staring at the television screen which now had only snow on it. My heart started banging in my chest. I broke out in a cold sweat, and remember having to concentrate as if I was talking to each appendage trying to get them to move. Slowly, the fingers and the toes started to move until finally like a flash flood my arms and legs stretched out from the fetal posture I was in and rolled over. I sat up in the midst of that cold wintry morning in Nu'uanu in our cottage flushed and perspiring trying to figure out what exactly had just happened. I didn't go back to sleep until the sun came up later that morning.

After my wife returned from her business trip, we were together in the living room watching the newscast at about 10:00 p.m. I looked over at Keola where he was sleeping on his bed under the bookcase and saw that he was again smiling in his sleep. I called to my wife to come and watch him with me. As we watched we were giggling, trying not break into a laugh so we wouldn't wake him. We felt a little guilty because it was like we were watching Keola smile and laugh in his dream without his knowing of our presence.

A week or two went by when this smiling and laughing episode happened again. Only this time the smiling had turned into a kind of smiling and a clicking noise as if he was sucking on his teeth. His head would also twitch and we noticed he stopped breathing. He was starting to turn blue!

"Keola! Keola!" my wife yelled out in horror. "Honey, get up! KEOLA!"

There was no response from our son, so I grabbed him and started to shake him a bit. Still he didn't respond. I gave him a slap on his cheek, trying desperately to wake him up. His eyes finally opened. He looked at us in disbelief, probably realizing what he had just dreamt, then started to cry and was afraid to go back to sleep. That night, Keola slept with mommy and daddy.

When Keola's strange behavior during his sleep started to reoccur, we took him first to his pediatrician. As his nighttime episodes continued with more frequency until they were occurring three or four times a week, the pediatrician referred us to a specialist in the neurology department at Straub Clinic. Our fear was that for some reason or other Keola could be having bouts with epilepsy while sleeping. After weeks of testing and brain scans and all kinds of tests that supposedly should have zeroed in on what was ailing our son, the doctors concluded that nothing was wrong with him. Not a thing!

I was outraged at the doctors. I started yelling at them that if nothing is wrong with Keola, why was this happening to him almost on a nightly basis?

"SOMETHING IS WRONG!" I started screaming right in the clinic. Later, I felt sorry for yelling at the doctors because they were trying their very best. They did care about Keola's condition. However, they simply had no answers.

My son witnessed my outburst and was frightened. As we left the clinic that afternoon, he took my hand in a firm little grip.

"Watcha going do daddy?" he asked me. I had no answer.

Then one morning the following week, the phone rang and I anxiously picked it up hoping to hear one of the Straub doctors on the other end saying they found out what was wrong with Keola. Instead, it was my mom. She gave me the address of this house that was no more than 5 minutes down the road from where we lived.

"When the doctors no work," she told me, "you better take Keola to see *odaisan*."

Odaisan, I thought, what was an *odaisan*? When my mom explained that she was a spirit-seer or priestess, I thought who needs spiritual mumbo-jumbo? Then I realized that I had nothing to lose even though I didn't believe in all this spiritual stuff. After all, the episodes were now becoming more frequent and seemingly more violent in nature and the doctors were still baffled.

I drove to the *odaisan*'s house within the hour after my mom had called. After I met this small, blind Japanese lady, the first thing I asked her was how I should address her. Was she some kind of *kahuna?*

"What ever makes you feel comfortable, James," she answered. "You can call me *odaisan...kahuna...*priest. I don't challenge those names nor waste my time with trivial matters, I just know what I do."

I immediately described the situation to her concerning Keola. The *odaisan* was very stoic, but possessed a kind of inner strength that I can't even begin to explain. She was very comforting and empathetic to my son's troubles. After I was done telling her all that I knew, she said nothing for a moment. Then she went over and knelt in front of the *obutsudan* or altar and started praying. When *odaisan* was done she came and sat next to me.

"The house you folks live in," she asked, "does it have a long driveway? Is there another house in front of yours that's on the same property? And is there one green lattice on the right hand side of the driveway with vines growing on it and does it has white flowers?"

My arms and the back of my neck were all chicken skin. *Odaisan* was describing the cottage where we lived and the house in front of us where the landlord lived. She went on to say that there had been an untimely death in the cottage and that she was getting images of an elderly woman in a wheel chair with a flannel blanket over her legs.

Odaisan then told me to return the following day. As I left her home I felt disturbed that these images of people or ghosts or *obake* or whatever you call those things—things that we can't see—were living in my home! Yet this simple Japanese woman who was blind could see more than I could with 20-20 vision! *Odaisan* would later tell me that at one time she could see, but, when she realized that she had this gift of seeing into the spirit world, she slowly lost her vision.

The next day before I was to go over to *odaisan*, I had some time to straighten out the small alcove where we stored all of Keola's toys. As I put things away, I came across a leather thermos holder that I had never seen before. It was a quart thermos holder and inscribed on the leather case in silver letters were the initials D.B. I don't really know why, but that afternoon when I returned to *odaisan*'s house, I brought the thermos holder with me. When I gave it to *odaisan* she nodded, made what seemed to be the sign of the cross over the leather case and then put it down. She never said a word about it ever again. *Odaisan* then instructed me as to what had to be done. After I received these secret instructions, I left.

When I got home, I was just going into the house when I noticed that my landlady was just pulling up the driveway. I greeted her and asked her a few questions about the cottage. I never told her anything about what had been going on in the house or Keola's strange episodes. What transpired during our conversation, however, next gave me a full-court press chicken skin!

My landlady told me a young nurse had lived in the house. She had been having personal problems and one day out of the blue, committed suicide by hanging herself. Well, I thought, for sure that was the problem. The nurse had hung herself by the corner with the bookcase over the bed that Keola slept on. It made sense according to what *odaisan* had said with a few exceptions. The main thing was that it was an untimely death.

However, the landlady had more. She then went on to say that before the nurse committed suicide, another tenant had died in the house.

"Poor thing, it was hard for her," the landlady explained, "especially after her son died of cancer. She was getting on in years. I remember when she fell down those stairs and broke her hip. After that she always had to be in a wheelchair."

"And what was her name?" I asked.

"Donna Bloom," she answered. "Every time it got cold, Donna had to put one blanket over her legs to keep it warm so it wouldn't ache so much." Now, you must remember that my landlord had no idea what was going on with the cottage and Keola. We never did tell her. But, as you can imagine, I went absolutely numb.

That late afternoon my wife and I started to do the things that *odaisan* told us must be done. First we had to sprinkle *pa'akai* or Hawaiian salt into all the corners of the house. Second, we had to repeat the Lord's Prayer while sweeping out all of the *pa'akai* through the front door. Then we had to burn a candle in the small alcove for 49 days without the candle ever going out. This ritual was rather tricky since religious stores sold slow burning candles which burned for only 12 hours. So to prevent the wind from blowing the candles out, we closed the window, kept the door shut and changed the candle every 10 hours just to make sure. There was one more thing that we had to do that night, but, *odaisan* told us that this had to stay with my wife and me for the rest of our lives and not to tell anyone. From that night on Keola's dream never returned.

A short time later when my wife and I went to thank *odaisan* for all she had done, she went on to say that sometimes when people aren't ready to leave this world, their spirits stay around and live, if you will, about 8 to 12 feet above the ground. However, *odaisan* believed that people who pass on should go into the spirit world and not hover near the living. Though it took a lot of energy from *odaisan,* this is what she was doing when she prayed at the *obutsudan* for Donna Bloom, to help open the door for her to move on.

"Spirits normally prey on younger children," she explained, "because they are virtually defenseless and so innocent."

Then she gave a piece of advice which I have always followed.

"If you don't know whose bed it was before you accept it," she told us wisely, "throw it out at the city incinerator. Don't just give it to somebody else. If you need a bed, buy one new one from the store."

Keola grew into manhood strong of body and mind. And I have never moved into a new house that I don't immediately replace all the mattresses. You never know what tragic tale unfolded on someone else's boxsprings.

THE HAUNTING OF H-3 FREEWAY

D uring the construction of the highly controversial H-3 across the island of O'ahu, stories begin to circulate in the community concerning unusual supernatural events which were taking place on this costly project. The path of the freeway cut into the undeveloped Halawa Valley on the leeward side of the island, bored through the Ko'olau mountains and then destroyed the scenic view of Haiku Valley with a ribbon of ugly cement. Beyond the political and environmental issues involved in the massive government project, many voices protested the fact that the freeway would destroy scores of valuable ancient historical sites. Native Hawaiian *heiau* or temples of significant value were being threatened. Even a curse had been placed on the H-3 construction project.

Deaths occurred during the construction due to freak accidents. A section of the freeway collapsed in the summer of 1996 in an area near one of the *heiau* being disturbed. Stories of "phantom hitchhikers" being picked up in Haiku Valley surfaced as an luminous spirit floating out of the hard rock of the Ko'olau mountain was seen by several workers inside the tunnel. Many of these stories were collected by cultural specialist Mahealani Cypher who one day will hopefully share them in detail with a wider audience interested in the spiritual dimensions of Hawai'i.

A few first-hand accounts of supernatural encounters have also come to my attention. During the placement of the special tiles which line the walls of the tunnel, one of the construction workers told me that he was busy with a small crew one early morning on the "graveyard shift." As they were securing the tiles into place, they all heard the distinct sound of a conch shell blowing. Looking toward the Haiku Valley entrance to the tunnel, they noticed a thick, white mist gently blowing into the tunnel. Inside that mist, the sound of the conch could be distinctly heard. Dropping their work, the men fled from the mysterious cloud which heralded the strange sounds of another world. It should be noted to the skeptics who have claimed that these workers created these "yarns" to get attention, that the person who shared this story quit his job. He took the risk of finding other employment over working on a project that he felt may be a desecration.

On another occasion, I met an engineer who had moved to Hawai'i from the East Coast of the U.S. so as to work on the H-3 freeway. He had had absolutely no background in Hawaiian history and culture, and knew nothing about the controversy surrounding the construction of the freeway. Ghosts had never bothered him in his very precise and calculated material world. Yet when he was doing the survey of the lands near the *heiau* in Halawa Valley, which was believed by Hawaiians to be an important female temple, he distinctly heard the sound of children playing in the sacred site. They were talking loudly to one another in a language he did not understand but could easily recognize—the Native Hawaiian language. When he went to see who was playing in the temple without authorization, he was shocked to discover that the area was absolutely empty of children, adults or any other living soul. Yet moments earlier, he distinctly had heard the young people speaking to each other in the ancient language of the Islands.

Following this incident, the engineer researched some of the cultural and historical concerns surrounding the H-3 freeway and decided to find another job. Like other people involved in the project who had had uncanny experiences, he believed it was far better to be safe than sorry.

When the freeway was opened to public use in 1998, the stories concerning its haunting began to circulate almost immediately. On the first week after the opening of the H-3, an individual called "Chicken Skin: The Radio Show" to report how he had been driving up toward the tunnel on the Halawa Valley side of the freeway when he had a flat tire. He pulled his car over just at the entrance to the tunnel. As he got out of the car to change his tire, he was greeted by a Hawaiian woman in a *kikepa* or *tapa* sarong worn under one arm and over the shoulder of the other. She was a friendly, middle-aged woman who spoke to him only a few words in English. He thought she was one of the Hawaiian activists whose many protests to the freeway he had been watching in the news. She reassured him that if he needed help, she was certain that it was on its way. Even before he could answer, another vehicle pulled over with its headlights bathing him and his automobile in a white glare. The other driver got out of the car offering assistance.

The driver then turned around to tell the Hawaiian woman that she had been indeed prophetic. However, to his surprise, she had vanished from the side of the road. Looking down over the embankment, he saw that there was no one anywhere to be seen. Curious, he asked the other driver if he had seen where the Hawaiian woman in the *kikepa* had gone.

"What woman?" the driver answered. He swore that as he pulled over to offer his assistance, there had been no woman standing on the side of the freeway next to the stranded motorist.

The most recent story which has been shared throughout the Internet involves a couple driving back one evening to Kailua on H-3 just a few months after the freeway opened. As they were driving along within the speed limit, the blue lights of a policeman's patrol car flashed in their mirrors. They were being pulled over, they naturally assumed, for some traffic violation. What in the world had he been doing wrong, the driver wondered as he looked for his driver's license, car registration and insurance card.

As the officer walked up to the car, the driver was about to plead innocent to having committed any traffic violation when the policeman leaned down and politely give some advice to the motorist.

"Sir," the officer said, "you should keep your children seat-belted in the back when you are driving. It is very dangerous to allow them to jump around like that in the back seat."

"What children?" the driver asked.

"The ones in the back seat that were playing around," the officer said, shining his flashlight into the rear area.

The young couple had no children. And as everyone could clearly see, there were no children in the back seat of their car! Even the officer was a bit nervous, having insisted that he could see children playing and jumping around in the seat as he pulled up behind their vehicle.

The whole incident could have been explained away as an optical illusion except for one small factor. In the morning following their mysterious encounter with the policeman, the husband got into the car and noticed on the back windows something which they would have never been able to notice the night before. The windows were terribly smudged from the inside with the pattern of dozens of little hands pressed up against the glass!

Nightmarchers at Mokuleia?
As Told by Masayoshi Hieda

Y ou're camping at Mokule'ia? Betta watch out, brah. Plenty kine *obake* out there."

The warning had come to Masayoshi Tomita in the summer of 1997 from one of his local friends with whom he often went surfing. Since he had come from Japan to live in Hawai'i in 1994 to study English, Masayoshi had made many such local friends who had helped him assimilate the island culture. Although from these friends he had become vaguely aware that the islands had many *obake* or ghosts, he himself had never had any paranormal experience. The prospect that camping at Mokule'ia may involve a ghostly encounter seemed interesting, but entirely outside the boundaries of his personal reality.

Several days later, Masayoshi and a few of his friends visiting from Japan were sitting on the beach at Mokule'ia, the evening sky clear with only a sliver of the moon visible as a cool breeze blew offshore. The warning that his local friend had given him about ghosts was long forgotten as the moon arched higher in the star-filled sky and everyone went to their tents to go to sleep. Masayoshi took no time drifting off to sleep as the hour approached 3:00 a.m.

It was less than thirty minutes later when he awoke to the sound of heavy footsteps outside his tent. Initially believing that the sounds belonged to one of his friends walking about the camp area, he tried to sit up only to find that it was impossible to move. A tremendous weight was pressing down on his chest. Unable to scream or move, the sound of the heavy footsteps circled his tent. Gripped in panic, pressed down to the ground, he was horrified when the footsteps seemed to enter the tent, stepping now directly next to him. His heart pounded as an invisible being with heavy feet slowly walked around Masayoshi's paralyzed body.

The sound of the mysterious footsteps suddenly vanished, as the pressure on his chest lightened. Believing that the entity had left, Masayoshi began to rise up when suddenly he felt what seemed to be a single foot stepping down on his chest. He was violently pushed back to the ground with a heavy weight that seemed to crush his chest cavity! This unbelievable weight lasted for only a moment, but the young man's heart was pumping so fast from fear that it felt it would literally burst. And then the weight vanished, releasing him from its oppressive burden.

Masayoshi's scream in the early morning still woke everyone up as he hysterically shared what had happened. Whether or not it was a dream was quickly settled when everyone looked at the T-shirt Masayoshi had been wearing during the terrifying encounter. The impression of a wet footprint was clearly visible on the young man's shirt.

What ghostly encounter had this student from Japan experienced at Mokuleʻia? In an area charged with the *mana* or supernatural power of the ancient people of Hawaiʻi, one could not escape the thought that this young man had been inadvertently in the pathway of *Ka huakaʻi Po*, the marchers of the night. What other explanation could there be?

THE SWEETEST *ODANGO* IN HILO

ilo in the old days, Yuriko Kariya remembers, was very different than today. The dusty lanes of wooden cottages on the outskirts of town were a bustling Japanese immigrant village filled with the sounds of children's laughter and the odors of Chinese sweet candles, steaming *manapua* and the pungent fish sold by old Sugihara-san. Since no doors were ever locked or windows shut, everyone generally knew each other's business.

How could Yuriko not have taken special notice, then, of the very sickly but pretty woman clad in a dripping wet, plain, light-blue *kimono* who appeared at the door of papa's store that rainy evening seventy years ago? Ah, a new picture bride, Yuriko thought, sent over no doubt for one of the Ola'a plantation men.

"*Irasshaimase*," Yuriko said in her very best Japanese, slightly bowing. Mama and Papa had always insisted that she act as politely as possible to customers.

"*Amae...mono...ga hoshii, kudasai,*" The woman whispered her request so softly that Yuriko had to strain to hear. The patter of rain and swirling wind filled the night air.

"*Amae...mono...ga hoshii, kudasai*" the stranger again whispered a little louder, bowing very low.

"*Hai!*" Yuriko sharply answered. If this pretty woman with the sad look upon a colorless face wanted something sweet, there was plenty of choice in Papa's store.

"*Amae...mono...ga hoshii, kudasai*" the women repeated in the same forlorn, soft chant. Her brown eyes now looking up at Yuriko were gently pleading.

Mama had made fresh *odango* with *anko* or bean jam filling just that afternoon. Carefully wrapping one of the treats, Yuriko handed them to the woman who gestured in great embarrassment that she had no money.

"Please, it is a gift," Yuriko said without thinking. A slight smile came to the woman's unhappy face and she bowed several times, uttering her thanks.

"*Domo arigato gozaimashita,*" floated in the dark air as the woman walked off along the muddy road. The heavy rains had softened to a slight mist which appeared yellow in the light from the kerosene lanterns burning in the village homes. Yuriko watched as the stranger disappeared into the blackness at the edge of the village.

Of course, Yuriko had no intentions to tell Mama or Papa of what had happened. They would not have approved of giving away *odango* to beggars.

When Yuriko came home from American school the next day, she heard her mother and father talking with the neighbors about a miracle that had occurred. "How mysterious is life!" Papa kept muttering.

A fisherman passing by a cemetery near the village had heard last night a terrible wail. Following the sound, he found a freshly buried coffin that had been unearthed by the heavy rains. Inside was a new-born, crying infant enveloped in the protective arms of its mother's *kimono*-clad corpse.

The mother during her seventh month of pregnancy had become quite ill and fallen into a coma. Believing that she and the fetus were dead, the husband and his fellow plantation workers had buried her. When she revived in her coffin, the horror of being entombed brought on a premature birth. The mother had suffocated about twenty-four hours before the fisherman had heard the cries of the infant.

"In the corner of the baby's mouth was found smudges of *anko*," Mama said in a hushed tone like it was the choicest gossip.

"Don't listen to gossip," Papa lectured Mama. "Where would the baby get *anko?*"

"Mama's *odango* is the best in Hilo, Papa," Yuriko volunteered and everyone laughed.

Later, Yuriko confessed to Mama everything that had happened that evening in the store. "The love of a mother is very great," Mama told her, "even greater than death."

The next morning they went to the temple to pray. The great bronze bell thundered at Yuriko's swing of the ringer, sending echoes through the void to the realm of spirits where a mother in a plain, light-blue *kimono* had found peace in the faint yellow mist.

T he psychiatrist called me in the fall of 1997 under the strict condition that I would not use his name or hospital location. Suffice it to say that he gave his background as a *haole* or Caucasian male in his early forties with a degree in psychiatry from a major East Coast ivy league medical school. Having lived in the Hawaiian islands for several years, he now practiced at a rural clinic where his patients encompassed all ages and ethnic groups to be found in the Islands.

During the summer, he went on to explain, he began to meet with a young patient and her mother who made regular visits to the clinic to treat what he described as a mild form of disassociation. The young woman of Native Hawaiian ancestry claimed to see a large shadowy human form with no distinct gender that appeared to move about her house during the night and day. Although she claimed that this large shadow wasn't threatening her, its presence was extremely unsettling. The doctor diagnosed her condition as an early stage of mental disorder and began weekly sessions so that the girl with her mother could explore the roots of her emotional discomfort.

During one of these regular morning sessions, the young patient's eyes suddenly went into what he described as a "visual tracking" pattern. In other words, her eyes seemed to be following something moving behind him where he sat at his desk. This was the first time that she had demonstrated such unusual behavior. Trying to get her attention, he kept asking her what she was looking at. She was totally impervious to his questions for over five minutes as her eyes fixated on something moving about the room. Finally she spoke.

"The shadow, doctor, followed me to the clinic. It is standing right behind you."

He admitted to me that even before she spoke, he was experiencing the strangest sensation—a feeling as if someone was actually standing behind him. Of course this could have been the power of suggestion, since the young woman's eyes had been tracking this object and they had for weeks been exploring various facets of her "shadow." Now, however, he literally felt the hairs on the back of his neck go up as chills of "chicken skin" tingled over his flesh.

This woman is good, he thought to himself. She is very good. She is sucking me right into her psychosis.

Trained to maintain his rational balance in such episodes, he kept his mind fixed on being calm as he asked her a few questions.

"Is the shadow good? Is it a friendly presence behind me?"

"No," she answered flatly.

"Is it evil? Does it want to do me harm?"

"No," she replied. "It is neither good or bad. It just exists."

At that moment a physical manifestation occurred in his office which nearly caused his heart to stop. In the corner of his room he had mounted a new CD/tape deck system which he was still learning to operate. The tape player had a complex reverse play button which allowed the tape to be played on the opposite side without having to turn it over. It would require pushing three buttons to turn on that function of the stereo— the power button, the play button and the reverse button which needed to be held down simultaneously with the play button. No one was anywhere near the stereo. However, as the young woman's eyes tracked her shadow to the corner of the office, the music in his tape player suddenly blared out on the reverse side. All three buttons had been depressed!

His rationality, his training and a healthy dose of fear now clashed head-on. Not wanting to feed his patient's psychosis, he didn't want to acknowledge to her anything which had just taken place. Instead, he calmly stood up, walked over to the stereo unit and pushed the "Off" button. Returning to his seat, he spoke softly and in an calm voice.

"Thank you for coming in," he said to the girl and her mother who was herself astonished. "Shall we meet next week at the same time?"

No one in the room made any reference whatsoever to the incredible event which had just taken place. The mother and daughter exited the room and made an appointment for a session the same time next week with his staff. The doctor returned to his desk to contemplate what had just occurred.

He was still trying to rationalize what had happened when within minutes his next appointment was ready to be ushered into the room. This woman took one step into his office, let out a blood-curdling scream, turned and ran from the clinic. Several staff members chased her down the road, finally calming her down and escorting her back safely to the doctor's office. She refused to go into the room again, however, claiming that as she had entered the door, she had been terrified to see a large shadowy figure standing behind the psychiatrist.

"How do you explain that, Glen," he confessed to me, "except that there was some entity in that office which turned on that stereo and appeared to both those woman. I'm a trained psychiatrist and this whole thing flies in the face of everything I've been taught."

Interestingly, a Hawaiian *kahuna* or priest was asked to bless the clinic following these events. He informed the doctor that the spirit that had attached itself to the young woman had come with her to the clinic that day, and the entity then stayed there. This spirit now haunted the clinic, not the girl. Several blessings, the doctor went on to explain, had been made of the building and more would be given on a regular basis until the *pilikia*, or the trouble, was resolved.

"If you are a psychiatrist working in Hawai'i," the doctor finally said, "the cultural context of your patient's mental health needs to be appreciated. Now I'm beginning to think it even goes further. Perhaps there is some unknown force going on here that I cannot fathom, but to which I must keep a very open mind."

The Legend of Morgan's Corner

The young couple had driven out on the old Pali Road to find a romantic place to engage in an activity which in those days was called "necking." Although they had heard that the hairpin turn called Morgan's Corner was a "spooky" place, their fear of ghosts was overruled by their passion. No doubt the windows of their car steamed up as the night passed uneventfully around them.

When it was finally time for them to drive back to Honolulu, the couple were surprised to discover that the ignition of their automobile would only make a faint "clicking" sound when they tried to start the engine. The boyfriend got out of the car, lifted the hood and jiggled the battery wires. The car still would not start. Something had to be wrong with the battery, he told his girlfriend. Or the ignition. At any rate, he had no choice but to walk out from Morgan's Corner to get help in town.

The night was exceedingly dark. The air was getting moist and the girl had no umbrella or sweater. They decided that she would be safer and drier if she waited in the car with the windows rolled up securely and the doors locked. The boyfriend assured her that he would be back within the hour.

Curling up on the back seat of the car, the girlfriend waited and waited and waited for her boyfriend to return. The wind had picked up that early morning, blowing the low hanging branches of the trees over the roof of the car. Thump, thump, thump, she could hear the branches banging lightly above her. In time the drizzles came as the roof received the gentle downfall. Drip, drip drip. The hour passed and then another hour as she finally fell into a deep, peaceful sleep.

"MISS! MISS!"

The calls of the policeman as he banged on her car door woke up the young girl just before sunrise. The sky was still black, because wasn't the darkest hour just before dawn? The policeman motioned for her to open the car door.

Following his instructions, she was just about to ask where her boyfriend was when the officer reached in, grabbed the girl by the shoulder and pulled her bodily out of the car. She was frightened by his rough manner and was sobbing as he put his arm around her, pulling her head against his shoulder where he pressed it tight.

"Don't look back, miss," the officer insisted as he rushed her to his patrol car. "For God's sake, don't look back."

If he was trying to protect her, the officer had perhaps made only one great mistake that morning. By telling her not to do something, it piqued her curiosity to squirm her head about within his grip, and to glance back at the automobile which had been only a few hours before a place of romance.

The car was caught in the white glow of the officer's patrol car headlights. Above her automobile, hanging in the tree, something moved gently back and forth, something which made a soft thumping sound as it lightly struck the roof. At first it seemed to be a thick, drooping vine that was grotesquely shaped to resemble a human being. Her eyes focused as she saw that it was her boyfriend, tied by his feet from the tree, his arms extended just long enough that the tips of his fingers dragged the roof of the car.

Although the rains had long before ceased, she could still hear the drip, drip, drip of some moisture striking the roof. This liquid, however, was not water running from the leaves and branches of the over-hanging tree, but droplets of blood oozing from the deep wound that had been inflicted on her boyfriend's neck. From one ear to another, someone or something had slit

his throat, draining him of his blood like a slaughtered pig hoisted up by his feet and gutted.

If a brave heart goes to this tree at Morgan's Corner at midnight, hugs its large trunk and looks up into the grotesque branches, the body of the hanging boy will mystically appear, swinging back and forth in his ghastly posture of death. And if you see that boy hanging, then you will not be able to let go of the tree! Your own body will be griped in a supernatural vise as you struggle uselessly to break away, your screams being drowned out in the demonic laughter which envelopes you as Death takes one more victim.

What would a collection of favorite haunted tales of Hawai'i be without a retelling of the legend from O'ahu's most famous ghostly site, Morgan's Corner? Famed for its Halloweenish setting that invariably creates shrieks of terror just by the very mention of its name, Morgan's Corner actually consists of two sites—one on the Nu'uanu and the other on the Kailua side of the old Pali Road. Both Morgan's Corners are distinguished by a sharp hairpin turn, overhanging trees that reach down like ghouls and a pitch-darkness on moonless nights.

The discerning reader may therefore inquire—which of the Morgan's Corners was the setting for the horrible murder of the boyfriend? When did this tragic death take place? Who were the young people involved?

Without trying to disappoint anyone who wishes to believe that the famous "boyfriend murder" at Morgan's Corner was a real historic event, the truth is that this is a very famous "urban legend" found in many cities around the world. For example, at Bachelor's Grove Cemetery, in Chicago, Illinois, the exact same story has been reported in several sources including Rosemary Ellen Guiley's *The Encyclopedia of Ghosts and Spirits*. Even the detail of the boyfriend hanging upside down by his feet, his fingers scratching the roof of the car as the policeman warns the girl not to look back, is precisely the same. Either the murderer of that boyfriend is a well-traveled serial killer who uses the same modus operandi in every city of the world as he piles up his mileage-plus coupons, or the bizarre tale of Morgan's Corner is only a rumor created by the most dangerous source of a ghost story, the FOAF (friend of a friend).

Not that strange things do not happen sometimes to people who tempt the legend of Morgan's Corner! One evening, for example, I escorted a small group of students from Hawai'i Tokai International College on a visit to Morgan's Corner on the Nu'uanu side of the Pali. After we passed the hairpin turn, we continued on a short way along the Nu'uanu Pali Drive, well beyond the last house. When we reached the distinctive "tunnel of trees" near the place where the road joins the Pali Highway, we pulled our three cars over and proceeded to take a small hike into the woods to get a better "feeling" for the area. After walking about ten feet, the students declined to go any further and insisted that we return to Honolulu. Their cocksure bravery had melted in the darkness of the Nu'uanu woods!

Getting back into our cars, all of the vehicles started up instantly except for the newest one—a brand-new Toyota which was only about one month old. The battery was evidently very much alive—the headlights, interior lights and radio all worked. The car had given the driver absolutely no previous problems. Yet when he turned over the ignition key, all we could hear was a simple "click." Over and over he tried the ignition, only to keep hearing this simple, dead "click."

It was now 1:00 a.m. and the thought of getting a tow truck out to Morgan's Corner seemed like the last thing in the world I wanted to do. We lifted the hood of the car, jiggled the battery connection and tried the ignition again. I felt at times like the "boyfriend" in the legend. Again all we heard was the "click." The car would simply not start. Twenty minutes later I made the decision to drive back in to town and bring back a tow truck.

Just before I drove off, one of the students who had been patiently waiting in the back of my car asked if I knew what was wrong with the Toyota. I told him that no matter what we tried, the car would not start. This young man then volunteered to take a look at the problem. He had experience with automobiles, he exclaimed as he walked over to the disabled vehicle. The hood was still up and the driver still getting nothing but a clicking sound, when the young student looked under the hood. He touched nothing.

"Brummm!"

The engine started right up! The young man had not jiggled any wires or twisted any cables. He merely looked under the hood and the engine ignited. I told everyone to get going back to town before the engine died, and all of us returned to campus without further incident.

On the way back to town, I asked the young man what he had done to start the car. He assured me that he had done nothing, but there was one precaution he had taken before coming on the "ghost tour" which he now explained to all of us. Unzipping his hip pouch, he brought out a bag of *pa'akai* or Hawaiian salt which he had purchased from the market that every morning. He had then had the salt itself blessed at a Shinto shrine to ensure its protective powers for the "ghost tour" that evening. The one person among us who carried blessed salt had been able to resolve the problem without even having to touch the engine!

The Toyota, we all later learned, was in perfect running condition when the student had his car checked at the dealer the next day. The battery and ignition were just fine and gave him no further problems. Despite our strange little mishap, Morgan's Corner remains for me nothing more than a place for urban legends. This location is nothing more than a dark parking lot for the imagination to get carried away in and for tales to be exaggerated and embellished through the enthusiasm of each storyteller.

...Oh, this hairpin turn of nightmares is one more thing to me. It is a place where I would never go alone at night.

A DOPPELGÄNGER IN KA'A'AWA

Mary Ann Namahala was busy in the kitchen that morning preparing the first lunch to be served in the new Ka'a'awa beach house located on the beautiful windward coastline of O'ahu. Her close childhood friend Charlie Richards had bought the land years earlier, but only recently had invested the money to build the cottage which he intended to use as a retreat during his approaching retirement years. Since Mary Ann and her husband lived in Kailua, they had driven out early that morning to prepare for the inaugural meal. Charlie who had given the Namahalas a key to the beach house, would drive out from Honolulu later in the morning with his wife. Everyone anticipated a great first day at the newly-completed cottage.

As Mary Ann started to put a chicken into the roaster, she noticed what she thought at first was her husband standing at the kitchen door. Quickly looking over, she saw Charlie Richards standing at the doorway. His manner was a bit gloomy, Mary Ann thought, and she was startled by his sudden appearance. Her friend was wearing a pair of light gray trousers and a dark gray, long-sleeve light cotton sweater. His face was expressionless except for just a touch of sadness which was very uncharacteristic for her usually ebullient friend.

"Hi, Charlie!" Mary Ann said cheerfully. "So we are having roast chicken for lunch. Is that okay with you?" She looked back to the roaster, set the time and turned back to greet her friend.

Only Charlie Richards was no longer standing in the doorway. Neither was he in the dining room or parlor. In fact, he was nowhere to be found inside the house.

Mary Ann found her husband outside tinkering around with some of the tools in the carport. He was about to plant some new shrubs and flowers around the house which he and his wife had brought out from Kailua.

"Where did Charlie go?" she asked her husband. "I can't find him anywhere."

"Where did he go?" her husband answered, puzzled. "He hasn't shown up yet. Aren't they coming out later this afternoon?"

"No, he's here," Mary Ann explained. "I saw him in the kitchen. Just now."

"Well, I didn't see him drive up," her husband answered. "And his car isn't here."

It was very peculiar for Charlie to sneak into the house and then vanish in such a manner, Mary Ann thought as she resumed her preparations for lunch. Maybe he had forgotten something and had to drive off, and her husband was to busy to notice his arrival or departure.

About one hour later, Charlie Richards and his wife arrived at the Ka'a'awa beach house as scheduled. He got out of the car wearing the same light gray slacks and dark gray sweater that he had been wearing earlier. Only his demeanor was far more fun-loving, like the "good-ole'" Charlie to whom Mary Ann was accustomed.

"I'm glad to see you are in a better mood," she off-handedly said as she helped Charlie and his wife unpack from the trunk some small bric-a-brac they had brought out to decorate the new home.

"What do you mean?" Charlie asked.

"Earlier, you seemed so gloomy," she explained. "But you seem in a great mood now."

"What do you mean 'earlier,'" he asked, looking at her a bit puzzled.

"When I saw you earlier this morning," she continued, "you looked unhappy. Like you had lost your best friend."

"When did I see you earlier this morning?" he now asked seriously. "Mary Ann, I don't know what you are talking about."

"Now, Charlie Richards, don't scare me!" Mary Ann said adamantly. "This morning you were standing in the doorway of the kitchen looking at me! You were wearing those clothes and you looked very sad. Quit fooling around!"

"I'm not teasing you," he insisted. "I just drove up a few minutes ago. I haven't been here all morning until just now."

His wife confirmed that at the precise moment Mary Ann Namahala saw Charlie Richards standing in the doorway of the kitchen in Kaʻaʻawa, he had been getting ready to drive out to the windward side of the island at his home in Honolulu!

What strange vision, then, had Mary Ann seen? It certain wasn't the ghost of Charlie since he was very much alive. She was convinced it wasn't her imagination or an hallucination since she described the exact clothing that he had been wearing to her husband before she had seen his attire. Charlie was wide awake at the time that he saw him on the other side of the island, so it hardly seemed a case of "out-of-body" experience. Was this a psychic vision of the future? And if so, what did it mean?

Mary Ann did not know the term *doppelgänger*, but her experience seemed a perfect description of these unusual "double-goers." The apparition of a living person that is an exact duplicate, even including details of dress, these spirit doubles in European tradition were believed to be visions of impending death. Had Mary Ann received an omen that Charlie Richards was about to die?

The weekend at the new beach house proceeded uneventfully after this strange occurrence. Everyone seemed to have a good time, although Mary Ann felt both frightened and puzzled by her vision. When she returned home on Sunday afternoon, Mary Ann immediately called her mother for advice. A wise *kupuna* who had been steeped in the old Hawaiian beliefs concerning spirits, her mother asked her to call Charlie immediately to inquire concerning his health. Had he been feeling ill or weak? If so, you must advise him to hold a large *luʻau* on his beach property, to make an offering of a pig to the spirits and to have the entire land and house blessed immediately.

Charlie confessed to Mary Ann that indeed, he had in the last few weeks been feeling very tired and run down. He had attributed his weakness to the fact that he had so much stress both at work and with the construction of the beach house. His doctors had prescribed vitamins and iron-enrichment for his blood, but his weakness persisted.

"Charlie," Mary Ann explained, "you need to have a big *lu'au* at your Ka'a'awa house. You need to *imu* a pig and make an offering to the spirits. You've got to do this for your own protection. That is why I saw your spirit in the house so sad and gloomy. You will die if you don't have the blessing and offering."

"Mary Ann," her old friend said defensively, "is this just some excuse you and your mom cooked up to have me throw you guys a party?" He laughed nervously.

"No, Charlie," she said in dead seriousness. "I'm not joking you. My mother told me that the spirits of old loved the *'aina*, Charlie. They loved it so much that their spirits never left it. They live in the land, Charlie. You built your house on their land, but you never showed them any respect. You never made an offering. So Charlie, they are taking a *pua'a*, they are taking a pig for their offering. Charlie, you are the *pua'a*. You are the offering."

Charlie Richards did precisely as Mary Ann Namahala and her mother advised. The *lu'au* was attended by all their friends and family and a giant pig was cooked in an underground *imu*. An Hawaiian priest did the blessing as a portion of the pork was given in honor to the spirits of the land. For the living had learned a very good lesson through the *doppelgänger* in Ka'a'awa—that if you neglect the spirits of the past, if you scar their land, dig up their bones or desecrate their memory, then your life will be filled with unending *pilikia* or troubles. If you however honor *ka po'e kahiko*, the people of old, and live in harmony with them, then your life will be blessed by their eternal presence in the Islands they so loved in life and now inhabit in death.

An Incident in a Graveyard

It was 3:00 a.m. on a beautiful morning in Manoa Valley as I sat in a car with several University of Hawai'i students who had joined me to spend the night in a graveyard. We were parked on the top of a knoll in the rear of this historic cemetery, quietly waiting there among the tombs of the elders for the fireballs, the phantoms or anything else that would go "bump in the night." This neighborhood graveyard was famed for its reputation as a haunted place, and in those days my enthusiasm to connect with the supernatural carried me away into some very silly situations. After been crammed into that car for a couple of hours with nothing strange or unusual happening, I was beginning to decide that this was one of the "silliest" moments of my career as a "ghosthunter."

I was sitting in the front seat of the car at the right passenger's door. Although the six of us had earlier been walking about the graveyard, by early morning we had returned to the comfort of the vehicle. Everyone was getting very bored, as the conversation turned to school, gossip and other mundane matters. I was occasionally looking across the graveyard, at this point expecting to see or hear nothing. From where we were parked, you could see across the entire cemetery down toward the lower part of Manoa Valley. A partial moon and streetlights illuminated the tombs which seemed to glisten like tiny balls of fire in the night. It was just about time for us to call it an evening, when I saw her walking through the graveyard.

She was a woman of normal height wearing a white gown that flowed softly to the ground. Over her head was a delicate white veil that shimmered in the moonlight. This lady in white was moving steadily, almost seeming to float about 100 yards away from where we were parked. She was walking in the lower part of the graveyard near some of the neighboring homes. I squinted my eyes to make sure that her presence was no optical illusion. This woman, I concluded, was very much real. She was obviously walking home early in the morning, using the graveyard as a shortcut. This definitely was a flesh and blood person, I convinced myself, when she suddenly disappeared at one of the tombs!

I never said a word to any of the other people in the car, but waited a moment to see her reappear, moving now in the opposite direction. She walked steadily back through the graveyard when she came to another tomb, and then vanished again! A moment later, she reappeared walking back in her original direction, reached the same tomb where she had first vanished and then disappeared again! As if through magic, she then reappeared, moving back through the graveyard where she again vanished at the same tomb. This lady in white was pacing back and forth between two tombs where she would dematerialize before turning and continuing her nocturnal walk. Was I losing my mind?

I calmly asked one of the people in the back seat for their flashlight. This was obviously a very clever optical illusion, I decided, that would be explained with the flashlight. I'd shine a light on the figure to determine if she were real or a figment of my imagination. Everyone in the car asked what was going on as I shined the light into the graveyard.

"Do any of you see anything in the graveyard?" I asked as the light bounced off the figure of the woman moving steadily along on her haunted path. This was definitely something in the cemetery and not an illusion.

"Yeah," the fellow next to me said, "it's a woman. She is going home through the graveyard. So what!"

"Watch her," I advised them, knowing what she was about to do when she came to a certain grave. As the lady in white approached the tomb, she gently vanished right before the terrified eyes of the other five occupants of the car.

Up until this moment, I had been exceedingly calm in my investigation of the lady in white. I had kept a rational mind operating, asking questions about her veracity, the nature of any optical illusions which may be operating or other natural explanations for this strange sighting. But when I heard the stark fear in my companions, I lost all control. Here we were purposefully visiting this place for the expressed intent of making contact with spirits of the dead, and now that we had one willing to cooperate, we were in pandemonium. All I could think of was a film that I had just recently seen at a campus cinema revival—the original version of *Night of the Living Dead*. The horror film opened in a graveyard where a couple watched someone walking among the tombs who turned out to be a flesh-eating corpse.

"GET ME OUT OF HERE!" I started screaming my head off, my heart-racing. "GET ME OUT OF HERE!" Tears were flowing down my cheeks as I banged on the dashboard, nearly cracking the plastic. "GET ME OUT OF HERE!" The wannabe ghosthunter had become a sniveling, sobbing coward. "GET ME OUT OF HERE!" The pounding on the dashboard was like drumbeats as everyone else was screaming with me. Outside, the lady in white continued her supernatural stroll.

The driver had not left his keys in the ignition, and was now groping in his pockets frantically to find them. In his nervous fear, he couldn't pull them out and I shifted my banging on the dashboard to banging on him. The person between us joined me in my pummeling of the driver.

"YOU IDIOT! GET THE KEYS! GET ME OUT OF HERE!" These impolite words were coming out of my mouth as the driver started using some interesting four-letter words better left out of the story. Then one of the back doors of the car opened!

"I want to get up close and see her," a voice of one of the guys in the back seat declared. "I'm going down there!"

"GET THE HELL BACK IN THIS CAR!" I screamed, reaching out of the window and grabbing the guy as he moved past me.

"Hey, let me go!" he screamed back, trying to break away. I used all my power to pull him into the front window, the top half of his body stuck into the car with his legs kicking out the side. The roar of the engine started as the driver found his keys and got the car going.

"GET OUT OF HERE!" I yelled again in what was becoming my spiritual mantra as a way to deal with this supernatural encounter.

I'm not certain what the acceleration rate of that car would have had to have been to get us out of that graveyard in two minutes, but we were literally flying out of Manoa Valley in the next few moments. Reckless driving would have been a polite term to describe our motion as we reached "civilization." The lights of the streets were blazing, a few homes had their front porch lights on, a couple of dogs barked and we pulled over, parked and started a long howl of laughter. It was a form of nervous laughter from a group of people who had just been terrified, but survived to tell the tale.

In fact, if events had ended there, this story would have been the first tale in this collection. It would have been titled "Stunning Proof of Ghosts." I would have "sworn on a stack of Bibles" that I had seen an apparition haunting the Manoa graveyard. The only problem is that the story doesn't end here. Once we regained our courage, we decided to return to the graveyard to see if the woman was still haunting her favorite tombs.

We stayed this time on the sidewalk near where the woman had appeared, prefering the streetlights to the darkness where we had been parked. Gazing into the exact area where we had seen the woman, we were a bit disappointed to observe that she had left. Obviously, she had achieved her purpose of terror and returned to the spirit realm. However, as we were leaving, we did hear something which we had not heard during our first encounter. It was a rhythmic sound coming from the area where the ghost had appeared—a mechanical clacking sound that in a few moments became very familiar to all of us.

In the backyard of one of the neighboring homes, someone at 3:00 a.m. had decided to water their small garden. Using a rotating lawn sprinkler with a powerful gush of water, they had set it in place with the pressure evidently on high. The sprinkler was clacking along as the water made its semi-circular motion. Only instead of watering the garden, the stream of water was overshooting the yard and spilling into the graveyard.

In fact, the water was hitting the very tomb where I had seen the woman in white make her first disappearance. At that point, the sprinkler reversed its motion and moved back through the graveyard, stopping exactly where the woman had vanished at the other tomb. In a moment it repeated its motion.

Looking directly into a high pressure stream of water at a distance, the top of the stream was narrow. As the water fell back to earth, it gradually expanded out, forming a broad mist that covered the earth. When the stream of water moved to the furthermost edge of its motion, the water was briefly not visible until it reappeared on its reversed path. Under a moonlight illumination in the middle of the night, the water shone with transparency, taking on the appearance of a veiled figure in a white gown.

In other words, we were all having heart attacks looking at a water sprinkler!

This story is shared as the last of the forty-nine tales in this collection not because I believe that all of the other forty-eight stories which precede it can be explained by water sprinklers, sheets hanging on a backyard laundry line or shooting stars that appear like fireballs. While some supernatural phenomenon may indeed be explained away under rational scrutiny, the stories themselves have a cultural and historical meaning that far outweigh the question of whether the occurrence was natural or preternatural.

However, if you are interested in answering the ultimate question—can the spirits of the dead communicate with the living?—then the proof of an afterlife must stand all the tests of reason and doubt. We need to separate natural causes and imagination from that single true supernatural event that stands as testimony that these bones can live again. The haunted water sprinkler tale doesn't undermine your faith that ghosts do exist. The story stimulates us to keep an open-mind—to keep our senses and our reason alert—as we patiently look for that one solitary shred of irrefutable evidence that beyond the grave awaits another as yet undiscovered adventure.